ISBN 979-8-9897701-9-9

Published by Hidden Hand Press
www.hiddenhandbooks.com

HIDDEN HAND PRESS

Ill-Gotten Things

BY Matt Bliss

CONTENTS

Little Silver Instruments   2

The Piano in the Basement   16

Screwed in the Head   36

Color Me Gray   40

What Face Will You Wear Today?   62

I Found It at the Record Store   75

Ripples of Psychosis   86

On a Sea of Shadows   90

Don't Eat the Candy   114

Loose Lips   129

A Life in Dust   146

Tooth and Nail   154

Stingers and Scratches   160

The Nights I Die   178

Grandpa's Magic Wishing Box   198

We Held Magic in the Woods   220

Little Silver Instruments

Jessica pressed her ear to the door, listening to her father's rhythmic whistling between the wasp-like buzzing on the other side. It was good to hear him happy like this—he sounded a completely different man while at work. Although her father had made it very clear that she was never to go down there, Jessica would tiptoe downstairs and shove herself to the door each night, just to listen to his joyful whistling. What Jessica never understood, however, was why her daddy kept his being a dentist a secret.

"Open wide," she heard him say, followed by a funny little chortle that sounded like a fluttering of notes.

She imagined herself a dentist too. Only seven years old but still wearing a long white coat. Rubber gloves stretched tight over her chubby little fingers. She could practically see herself working nimble tools across ridges of teeth. When she grew up, she reasoned, she would do this too. She would become a dentist, just like her dad.

"Has anyone told you that you have a lovely smile?" He laughed again.

Jessica liked that laugh. She wondered why he had never laughed like that when she was around. Maybe she wasn't funny. Or... maybe it was some sort of grownup laugh. Like when she heard teachers talk behind flattened hands, or the mailman when he lingered too long at Miss Holdstien's doorstep. Only this laugh was different. It sounded like it came from deep in her father's belly. A contagious little sound, and Jessica often pinched her lips to stop herself from repeating it.

"Good... just about done. One more and we'll get you back home in no time at all." Metal chimed as it clattered against the basement floor.

He sounded so calm like this, Jessica thought. So in control. Nothing like the daytime Dad she knew. The one who would snap at her wrists when she moved too close. The narrow stare he held until the clouds passed from his sky-blue eyes. It must be hard, she thought, to keep a thing you love so much a secret. Jessica could hear that love through the door. If she focused her ears hard enough, she swore she could hear him smile.

Something thudded to the floor with a heavy whump. Jessica could feel its weight against the concrete.

"SHIT!" her father shouted. His pleasant voice was now a feral growl. A familiar warning from a wild-eyed beast. Heels clicked across concrete—he grumbled, then panted for breath.

Time to go. Jessica turned and hurried back to her room, careful to step on the outside stairs so they wouldn't squeak. She eased her bedroom door shut and slipped beneath her covers, falling asleep only moments after tugging blankets to her chin.

That night, she dreamed of gleaming white smiles and sparkly clean teeth. Somewhere in the darkness, she heard her father whistling along with his joyful little tune.

* * *

Jessica blew out her breath as the school bus screeched to a stop outside. The door collapsed, and the driver watched her for a moment, chewing furiously on a wad of gum. "Well..." he said, raising his palms above him. "We can't do this every day, darling. Are we getting on today?"

Jessica clenched her fists and released them, and climbed the four tall steps before her.

Twenty pairs of eyes all fixed on her, and the heat of it made her squirm. She sidled past, eyes scanning from one seat to the next until they finally stopped on a girl she didn't recognize. She had curly red hair, more freckles than a night sky, and the most perfect smile she had ever seen.

"You can sit with me," the girl said, tucking herself against the window.

Jessica slid into the seat and looked again at the girl's smile. It was flawless—even for a kid her age. Porcelain white and as symmetrical as a butterfly's wings.

The girl shoved out a hand. "I'm Samantha. It's my first day here. My old friends called me Sam."

Jessica grabbed her hand and gave it a quick shake. "I'm Jessica. My friends call me... well, I don't really have any friends, but Jessica is fine."

The boy in front of them, Michael Riggits, let out a spit-choked laugh.

"Well, it's nice to meet you."

Jessica smiled and looked again at the girl's perfect teeth.

Sam noticed her gaze and held a hand over her lips. "I don't have something in my teeth, do I?"

Jessica blushed. "No, sorry... I just think you have nice teeth. My Dad's a dentist and I—"

Michael suddenly burst into a fit of laughter. "No, he's not!" he said, swinging around toward the two of them. "He's a janitor! My dad sees him at the hospital all the time. Says he's weird, and a liar, just like you." His head cocked back and forth with the last three words.

"He *is* a dentist! And he's not weird, and I'm not a liar."

"What kind of dentist mops puke off the floor?" He laughed again. It was a mean sort of laugh, one that echoed through the shell of the bus and turned everyone toward the sound.

Jessica wrapped her arms around herself and tucked her chin to her chest.

"It's okay," Sam said, placing a hand on her shoulder. "I believe you." She glared daggers at Michael instead.

But Jessica jerked away, and remembered exactly why she hadn't tried to make friends sooner.

* * *

Jessica got home, curled up into a ball, and cried. She wanted her father there, to comfort her, to tell her friends he was a dentist, and that mean boys like Michael Riggits are just big dumb dummies who wouldn't know the difference between a molar and a mop until the handle knocked him upside the head. But as usual, the house was empty. He wasn't that kind of a dad anyway.

All day, she had had to listen to Michael and his goons laugh at her. They called her a liar and said terrible things. Sam, as kind hearted as her smile, had tried to help, but it wasn't fair to her. It was Jessica's problem—she had to handle it. So when Michael stuck his pointed chin in her face, and brought the tip of his tongue to his two crooked teeth, ready to say that word again, Jessica balled up a fist, reared back, and threw it into his face.

He staggered back in surprise. Michael touched a finger to his lip, pulled it away with a smudge of bright crimson, and wailed like cicadas in summertime. Teachers came, marching Jessica to the office and placing her in the hard plastic chair where she *simply must explain herself*. When she did, they took Michael's side. He is going through a really hard time at home right now, and he's just lashing out. Whatever that's supposed to mean.

It wasn't fair, and as Jessica wiped warm tears on the sleeve of her shirt, she decided she would prove it to them all. She would show them she wasn't a liar.

Jessica stomped down the stairs to the basement. This time aiming for the steps that squealed in defiance. She jostled the handle, and to her surprise, it opened. Jessica had been in there before. Daddy wasn't very good at making sure he locked the door, and he trusted Jessica to listen, but who needed to listen when you're being laughed at in school?

She snapped on the light, and the room came to life exactly as she remembered it. A vinyl padded chair sat in the center of the room, just like the one her own dentist had. It could recline or lay flat, turn or sit up straight—just about whatever you wanted it to do. Above it, a round lamp hung connected to a spindly arm. The kind that blinds you and makes you see spots when you close your eyes. Surrounding the chair were trays lined with gleaming silver tools.

If he weren't a dentist, why would he have these?

Jessica climbed into the chair and laid back. "Open wide," she remembered hearing Daddy say, and she opened her mouth, imagining the tiny little mirror moving around inside her mouth. Her cheeks pulled back in a smile, making it impossible to hold her mouth open. Most kids feared the dentist, but not Jessica. It was her calling, after all, and she would be the one holding the tools when she was old enough.

She hopped off the chair and ran her fingers over the little tools, listening to them tinker as they touched one another. She considered taking one—bringing it to school to show Michael and the others, but she could jam it in Michael's eye and he still wouldn't believe her.

She turned instead to Daddy's desk in the corner. An old thing, marked with deep gouges and a bulky computer about just as old on top. Rows of shelves stood behind it, overflowing with files and papers, and a neat row of VHS tapes alongside them. He marked each one with a patient name, age, and a note. Beyond it stood a clothing rack, filled with an assortment of shirts and dresses. Different sizes and styles, and Jessica could only think they once belonged to her mother. That's why Daddy couldn't part with them, she reasoned. Some were her size, however, and on days when Daddy was gone, Jessica would dress up in them. Her favorite was a much too big lemon yellow dress. She would dance around the chair, whistling Daddy's cheerful tune, spinning faster and faster until the dress poofed out like a flower blooming in spring.

Jessica plopped down on his desk and looked at the mess strewn across it. A folder lay on top, and Jessica pulled it closer to read the words written across its cover.

Sarah Riggits. Age: 36. 5/5, best one yet!

She thought about the name, and why it sounded familiar. Michael's last name was Riggits too. She laughed loud at the thought. Michael's own mother was one of her dad's patients. She must have a wonderful smile, she thought while reading the handwritten comment, and that made her think back to Sam's perfect smile. She would say that was a five out of five smile as well.

Jessica worked a finger underneath the cover to open it, but just before peeling it back, she heard the unmistakable sound of the front door swinging open and shut.

Jessica shoved the folder under her shirt and tucked it into the back of her waistband. She hurried to the stairs, listening as Daddy's footsteps thumped into the kitchen. Slowly, she snapped off the light and eased the basement door shut. She moved upstairs, careful to step on the outside steps like she did every night. Once she found her backpack, Jessica smuggled the folder inside. She had the proof she needed, to show she wasn't a liar, and her father would never know. Jessica smiled wide, showing each and every tooth.

***

At school the next day, Jessica could hardly contain herself. She knew Michael would turn his overbite toward her and let loose another flurry of insults. So when the teacher wasn't looking, and Michael finally did turn to Jessica with his tongue pressed to the tip of his two crooked teeth, Jessica only smiled in return.

"Go ahead," he said. "Smile away like a little liar. We all know what you really are."

Sam pointed a chin between the two. "If you say that again, I'm going to have to tell."

He wiggled his fingers, letting out a ghostly sound before turning back to his own desk.

"I believe you," Sam said. "And I think if you want to be a dentist someday too, you'll make a great one." She smiled, revealing those perfect teeth once again.

"Thank you, Sam."

"I doubt he's ever even gone to a dentist with teeth like that," Sam snickered.

Jessica scanned the class for watching eyes and reached inside her bag. "Want to know something funny?" she asked, removing the folder from her bag like a blade from its sheath. "I found this in my dad's files."

She slipped it over to Sam's desk and tapped a chubby finger on the name. "I think it's Michael's Mom."

Sam's eyes went wide and she let out a single note laugh.

"All this time he made fun of me, but really my dad is his mom's dentist!"

The girls giggled behind flattened fingers, and Michael snapped his head back to the sound.

Jessica watched as Sam turned open the folder, and her perfect smile suddenly faltered.

Sam took one gasping breath and screamed.

The class spun round and watched as she continued to shriek. She sprang up, shaking, swatting at herself as if covered in ants. The folder fell to the floor and photos spilled out from inside. Square images, dancing through the space like leaves in the wind before falling flat.

Michael screamed next. Tears welled in his eyes and his bottom lip quivered. Then, a word worse than liar leaked out. "Mommy..."

One by one, the sound of terror spread through the class until the entire room was sick with it. Jessica looked down and recoiled from what she saw.

There were dozens of them.

Photos of a woman with marbled gray skin. Her face was slack and twisted. Her eyes were milky white. In some photos, she wore the clothes that hung on her father's rack. The same lemon yellow dress she had danced in, spinning faster and faster until the ruffles bloomed, now draped over this woman's cold splotchy flesh. In other photos, she wore nothing at all, with her limp body posed in lurid ways. In those, Jessica's own father was right there with her. Holding her, and using the little silver instruments.

Jessica knew then—her father wasn't a dentist—he was a monster.

* * *

The patient looked up at Jessica and twisted his face in recognition. He wasn't the first person to recognize her. There were plenty before him who knew her face from newspapers. The girl who didn't know... and each time they wanted to bring up that painful past in horrific details.

She pulled on her gloves and smiled at the satisfying snap of latex. She loved that sound. Just hearing it sent a special little thrill through her nervous system, equal to the purist dopamine rush money could buy. Not only that, but it told both her and the patient of what's coming next.

"Let's take a look," she said and adjusted the light until her patient squinted and turned toward her.

"Wait... aren't you—"

Jessica shoved the tiny silver mirror deeper in his mouth to silence him.

"Eww arrr," he said, keeping his mouth open and tongue pressed back.

"You haven't been flossing, it seems." She removed the tool and held her unwavering smile above him. "You have some cavities, too. Lower right second and third molars."

The man watched as she reached behind him, pressing her face close to his and squeaking knobs in back of the chair.

"I remember you," he said, trying to lift himself from the chair, but Jessica lowered him back with two fingers to his chest.

She reached for the cylindrical steel drill beside her and revved it beside him like a sports car at a stoplight.

"Yeah," the patient said. "From the news a while back. Your dad was that janitor at the hospital... the one who took the bodies home and—"

"Open wide," she said, followed by a funny little laugh that sounded like the tinkering of metal.

"You were the one," He flinched away with eyes wide enough to park planes in. "You're the reason he got caught. Christ, all those people... all those years and women and kids even... All those pictures you found and took to school, all because you thought he was a—"

"A dentist, just—like—me." Jessica pressed the plastic mask on top of his nose and mouth, and couldn't hear him over the bitter hiss of gas leaking out. "It wasn't all that bad, you know. Had it never happened, I never would have followed my passion to become a real dentist." She still held the smile as his eyes rolled back and his body went slack.

She reclined the man back and danced around him, spinning until her long white coat bloomed like a flower in spring. Then she plucked a gleaming silver tool from its tray, and her nimble fingers worked the sharpened edge beneath each button along his shirt. She sliced them free, sending the little plastic pieces pinging across the room and his shirt peeled open, exposing soft flesh.

"Open wide," she said, and laughed from somewhere deep in her belly. And somewhere in the darkness behind her, she heard her father whistle his joyful little tune.

The Piano in the Basement

F irst off, I hadn't even done anything. Well, I had, but I had been defending myself, you know? It wasn't my fault he was half my weight and had dropped like a sack of rocks after one punch. That was what you got for picking on the fat kid. Band geeks could throw punches, too—even if Jared Simons hadn't known that. I bet he knew that now though, and he'd probably think twice before calling anyone else a lard-ass and poking them in the belly.

Either way, forty hours of community service seemed a bit unfair for standing up for myself. They'd made me do one of those "Scared Straight" programs where a group of convicts got in your face and yelled at you about their poor life decisions and how if you kept going down this road of self-destruction, you were going to end up *just, like, them.*

I thought I was already scared straight before that— straight A's, honor roll, math club, and what have you, but they didn't care about that. If you looked a certain way on paper, people thought they knew you. Came from the bad side of town, no father, mother had died of a drug overdose... trajectory plotted directly toward a prison sentence by the time he was twenty-one. X equals doomed to repeat the sins of my father.

My counselor said I wasn't quite suited for the more strenuous volunteer options, like picking up trash on the side of the highway, and instead suggested the Senior Home Services program. "You have the right personality for it," he said. Whatever that meant.

"What do I have to do?"

He pulled a pamphlet from the overflowing pile of paperwork on his desk and handed it over. The front showed a picture of a smiling teenage boy standing next to a happy old man in a wheelchair with a hand on his shoulder.

"Volunteers spend time assisting one of our elderly community members in their homes. It could be helping with meals, cleaning up a bit for them, or just hanging out and talking. Whatever they want or need help with."

This seemed a heck of a lot better than wearing an orange safety vest and swinging a trash poker in the sun so I agreed. Forty hours of reading to old people didn't sound all that bad.

Oh, how wrong that thought turned out to be.

***

The house was the same pale blue as the sky. It blended in like camouflage as if to say, Nothing strange is going on here. Just a normal, small, middle-class suburban house like all the others on the street.

They hadn't told me anything about the assignment. Nothing about who lived there, what they wanted, or what I would have to actually do to help them. On top of being fat, I had some serious anxiety issues, so stressing out about this Pandora's box of suck was just another part of the punishment, I supposed.

The wooden steps moaned as I plodded up to the porch and rang the bell. I heard the front door open, but they had a screen door that shrouded the person behind it in darkness.

"What do you want?" a voice grumbled from inside.

I squinted and shifted my head, trying to see past the screen to who, or what, was standing behind the doorway, but I could only make out blobs of pale flesh.

"Hello, sir, or ma'am. I... I'm sorry to disturb you, if I did, in fact, disturb you anyway, but I'm Wesley." I rocked on the balls of my feet, rubbing the palms of my hands against one another fast enough to start a fire.

The voice didn't speak back.

"I'm a volunteer with the Senior Home Services program. I'll be here to assist you today. If you want assistance, I mean. Or if there's someone else in the home who needs assistance in there. I really don't know... but you know... So, I, uh... sorry."

They let out a long, wheezing sigh. "Right, volunteer. Come on in."

A pudgy arm propped the door open, and I stepped inside. She was a large woman with a bird's nest of silvery hair. I sucked in my gut to shimmy past her and her vomit-green nightgown.

"First things first," she said, thumping the door shut behind me. "I expect you to be here by four o'clock on the dot until you are told otherwise. You will vacuum the entire downstairs before polishing the furniture and dusting all the shelves. There will be no snack breaks, bathroom breaks, or smoking while inside my house. Do you understand?"

Her skin hung from her face like the floppy ears of a dog. I nodded.

"Then, you will move onto the bathroom, where you will mop the tile, scrub the toilet, and polish the brass handles until they shine. Clear?"

Again, I nodded.

"Only when you are done with that will I sign your hours' sheet. If you break my rules, I won't sign a thing. Got it?"

"Yes, ma'am, Miss..."

She looked at me sideways. "Henley," she said, and the corner of her wrinkled mouth turned up only the slightest. "You might actually have a little respect in you, it seems. Not like the other hoodlums and troublemakers they've sent. I like that."

I fidgeted in my shoes. "Thank you, ma'am."

"Well, get to it now. The vacuum is in the closet." She motioned to a door at the base of the stairs, gripped an extra-wide walker, and shuffled off in a trail of labored breaths.

This, I thought, was going to be the longest forty hours of my life.

The vacuum had to have been older than its owner, and it wheezed just as hard, too. It didn't help that the splotchy shag carpet looked like it hadn't been vacuumed since Jimmy Carter had been in office. For someone who wanted their house so spotless, they sure didn't mind living in filth.

Every time I thought I was done, Mrs. Henley pointed out the nooks and crannies and other areas that weren't quite to her satisfaction. "Are you blind or just stupid?" she asked me.

I didn't answer.

I went through seven rags and nearly passed out from the amount of lemon-scented furniture polish I used. My fingers wrinkled then split, and the cuts burned from the oily chemical seeping inside. I dusted, cleaned, and organized, and only halfway in, I was more whipped than a carnival pony.

As I went to put the vacuum back in the closet, I knocked over a box stacked beside it, and the contents spilled out before me. I stooped down to put them back in the box when I noticed a picture in a frame. It was old, black and white, with a young woman, cheeks full and smiling with her arm around a man pressed close to her cheek.

"What are you doing?" Mrs. Henley asked, and I looked up to see her scowling above me.

"I was just picking it up."

"Don't touch that!" She quickly snatched the picture from my hand and pressed it to her chest.

"I'm sorry. I—"

"Take that box into the basement. And don't you go snooping through another one of my things, you hear?"

I nodded and carried the heavy box with me.

Thirty-six hours, I told myself.

The basement door opened to a set of stairs disappearing into the darkness below.

I swallowed hard and moved inside. Every part of me was sore. Muscles I hadn't even known I had ached, and evenwalking was painful. *Thirty-five hours and fifty-five minutes*, I reminded myself, counting down every bit I could.

Stale air punched me in the face as I descended the staircase. The scent moved around me almost as if the room was breathing— a throat leading into the belly. I slid my shoulder along the wall, lowering down with each cautious step. I touched toe first to the step below me, listening to it moan and heave beneath my bulk. Once it held, I moved to the next. It was darker with each step down, and at some point, light ceased to exist entirely.

I squeezed the box with one arm and swiped against the peeling wallpaper until I found a switch.

A bulb buzzed to life in a hazy orange glow and roaches were scattered across the bare concrete floor. The entire space was damp and empty except for one seemingly out-of-place object.

An old piano stood at the center of the room.

It was an antique upright with tapered spindles for legs, and seafoam green paint that peeled from its surface in dime-sized flakes. Every surface had been intricately carved with a floral pattern. Vines and leaves wrapped from one side to the other in deep set etchings that would be impossible to reproduce nowadays. Despite the age and disrepair of the thing, the workmanship was still striking. A true testament to its long forgotten creator..

I glanced over my shoulder for one last look at the door above before setting down the box and approaching it.

The piano felt like an actual living thing. A tiger crouched, ready to strike at any moment.

I reached for the keyboard cover that lifted with only a light touch, snapping up in a cloud of dust that swirled in the amber light. My fingers swept across the keys —ice cold. They had an almost metallic feeling, nothing like the pianos I had known, and they pulled at my hands as if magnetically.

The thought of my mother came back for some reason I couldn't explain. It had been her who'd wanted me to take piano lessons. This was way back before the drugs had sunk their crippling claws deep into her. She'd thought if I did something like that, something fancy like the happy white families on television, everything else would fall in line too. Maybe I could have a small piece of that life. Maybe we wouldn't be doomed to a life in a bad neighborhood.

I hadn't wanted to play at first butMomma had forced me to. Made deals with the neighbor for lessons and practices until we'd somehow got a piano of our own. She'd said I would thank her someday, but when she'd died, I hadn't felt thankful one bit.

I pushed my thumb and ring finger down in the root position. Despite its age, the keys somehow still felt springy, and the low note rattled through me with a warm bass chord. My lips curled back in a smile.

"Do you play?"

The voice rang out from the top of the stairs so suddenly, I jumped back and caught my heel on the box I'd set down. Mrs. Henley stood halfway up the staircase, holding one hand to the wall beside her.

"I'm sorry, Ma'am. I was just leaving the box and—"

"Do you play?" she asked again. Unlike earlier, her face was calm, almost expressionless.

I swallowed a dry mouth. Still startled, I hadn't even heard her coming down the squeaky stairs. "Yes," I said. "My mom made me play for her when I was younger."

I furrowed my brow, wondering why I was telling her this.

She nodded, and an uncomfortable silence hung between us. "Play something," she finally said.

"I really don't think—"

"Please... Play something, please."

I blinked away the confusion and turned toward the piano with its flaking green paint. I could feel her expecting eyes on me as I dragged out the bench from underneath and eased onto it with the wood groaning underneath me. My hands hovered above the keys, and I wiggled each finger in anticipation, feeling that magnetic pull again. "What song do you want me to play?" I asked, still staring at the hard flatness of the keys.

"You know the one," she said.

An icy chill ran up my spine, and my fingers spread, pressing into the keys before I knew what was happening. They curled and spread and danced over the surface all by themselves. And what I heard, the song they played, was like nothing I'd heard before. Slow and sweet, in the warped pallor of strings that desperately needed to be tuned. My left hand struck thick chords while my right fluttered like a butterfly over the high keys.

The room shook around me. A wind rushed up from nowhere, flowing toward the wall at my back, pulling at the air with each note I played.

I played faster, feeling the sound move through me with an electric current. There was no stopping it now. I was no longer in control. The thought was terrifying, but I didn't want the music to end. I didn't want the melody to stop. My fingers worked faster, and the sound poured from them.

The air pulled at me harder—whistling in my ears, gasping at each feverish note like a drowning victim breaking the surface. Paint peeled off the piano around me and disappeared into the vortex of air. Flakes of green sucked away in a blizzard of seafoam paint.

I tried to pull back, to let the wind rip my hands from the keys, but I couldn't. The piano wouldn't let them.

The lights flickered, and darkness pressed at the edges of the room. A noise, a hiss, escaped from the walls around me, and for a moment, I thought the whole house was lost to the storm. I played faster, feeling each note walk along my flesh, and I wanted to scream.

Something moved closer to me. Still sucking the air, hungry for the music, and raising every hair on my neck. I could feel it there, breathing on me. Running long fingers across the back of my hair. Whispering to me.

Play more, it said. Play me your sadness. Play me your pain. Show me your dreams that are yet to come true.

And in the pallid darkness pulling at my mind, I remembered my mother. I had been so young then, so ignorant as she'd sprawled across the couch behind me. "Play for me, baby," she'd said, slipping between worlds of consciousness and the abyss. So, I had. I'd played, not because I wanted to, but because I had to, and the sounds had blocked out all the noise in the world, just as it did now.

I stopped fighting the thing surging through me. I let go and trusted my hands to dance like spiders on hot plates of ivory. Letting the thing behind me breathe and gasp and fill itself with each beautiful sound and painful memory that my fingers could show. Each soft line drawn with notes to show a picture of the woman with dark lips and eyes so generous you could crawl into them. A face I tried so hard to forget but couldn't.

The thing behind me throbbed with excitement. It tasted each vibration of the taut strings and the memories resonating within it. It plucked them from me one by one.

My back grew tight, and the darkness pressed closer, threatening to pull me under the warm sheet of blackness. It twitched and shivered and finally let out a howling scream equally as loud as the music.

Then, as suddenly as it came on, my hands stretched and struck a final chord. It rang loud in my chest. A perfect crescendo to an orchestra of madness.

The air settled with a whump, and my ears popped as normalcy returned. The light returned to its amber glow, swinging slowly overhead as I remained paralyzed, still staring at my fingers, expecting them to move. Yet, they didn't. At least not on their own.

Tears splashed down on top of them, warm and slick, and I knew they were my own once again. I wiped my sleeve across the wetness on my face and turned behind me.

Nothing.

Only a yellow wall and splotches of dark mold. Beyond that, however, still standing halfway up the stairs, was Mrs.

Henley. She held the wall the same as when she found me, but now she looked different. Her eyes sparkled, and her face, now glistening with tears, had softened. The forked lines around her eyes pointed up, the edges of her lips pulled into a thin smile, and the wispy gray hair glowed with a golden hue. For a moment, I swear she looked as young as the girl in the photo I found. She looked just as happy.

She turned and teetered a moment on her feet. "My love…" she said, and suddenly, her knees buckled.

I jumped to my feet and sprinted toward the stairs, but it was too late. Mrs. Henley dropped to the stair below her, shins cutting into the stair's edge, and tumbled backward down the stairs. The sound was like a drum solo, but each thump and bang was her head or arms or hip hitting the wall or stairs until one last bang signaled a stop.

I ran to her side and cradled her head as she blinked up at me. She still wore the unnaturally wide smile on her face as her eyes rolled back in her head.

* * *

It wasn't long after I called that a paramedic arrived. Blood had soaked through my sweatshirt by then, and though it was difficult for them to get her out of the basement, they managed it rather quickly.

"She just fell?" one asked me over the hiss and pop of Velcro as they strapped her to the gurney.

I nodded but looked toward the piano.

She was breathing but unconscious when they took her away. And I could just tell from their reaction that it wasn't good. She was old, and sometimes, a fall down the stairs was enough.

I walked home alone, thinking it over, blaming it all on myself. It was my fault. I mean, how couldn't it be? I played the piano while she just stood there. She was there... because of me. Because of that damned piano and that damned thing telling me to play.

I could feel it then, breathing on my neck, lifting each little hair on my arm with its hot breath in my ear. A voice familiar but not. A thought that made me want to squirm, but I reached out to it anyway. It didn't make sense, and it couldn't have existed, yet the memory was clear. The wind. The song. The memories it had pulled from me—memories of... something...

I struggled then to see what it was. Play for me, baby. The words seemed far away and forgotten. A ghost of chalk on a blackboard wiped clean.

And as the days passed, with no word about Mrs. Henley, it seemed all I could think about was that piano. The smoothness of the keys, the long hum of sound ringing from inside; the paint stripping away like a snake shedding its skin.

A week later, I dreamed of the piano. It was a living, breathing thing. Its heartbeat hammers on strings; its pulse pumping beneath my fingers. It called to me. It spoke to me. Wanting me to feed it, so it could grow, so it could survive. And somewhere inside me, I truly wanted to feed it. All those terrible memories that came back. The things I kept secret from the world. The things that made my eyes wet, my heart ache, and stole my breath... I wanted to turn them into something beautiful. To feed them to this thing and let melodies ring forth instead.

I tried other pianos after that, keyboards too, but nothing sounded like it had in the basement. I had to go back. I had to see it and feel it purr beneath the gentle touch of my fingertips.

The house was quiet when I finally went back. I stood outside the pale blue house for an eternity, training my ear to anything moving inside, but heard nothing. I plodded up to the porch like I had weeks before and rang the bell. This time, I wasn't anxious or scared. I was excited.

No one answered. I pulled open the screen door and knocked. Still, no one answered.

I reached out and wrapped my hand around the doorknob. As I turned it, I could feel the mechanisms inside shift, and the door opened freely. It was unlocked.

"Hello," I called out, poking my head inside. "Mrs. Henley? Are you here?"

Nothing answered, and suddenly, I feared the worst for her.

I eased the door shut behind me and padded across the thick carpet toward the basement door. The light was still on, exactly as I'd left it, and I stepped down toward the dark stain at its base.

"I had a feeling you'd come back."

I looked up to see Mrs. Henley sitting at the piano bench in the center of the room. She seemed to glow in the amber light. Still smiling with sparkling eyes like I remembered before she fell.

I swallowed hard and tried to return my eyes to their normal size. "Are you—"

"I'm fine, dear. It could have been much worse, really." She patted the spot on the bench beside her. "Come. Sit."

I moved toward her on shaky legs and sat beside her. The piano seemed to watch my every move.

She looked toward it and sighed. She seemed healthier now. At peace. So much different from when we'd first met.

"What... happened?" I asked. "I mean, I knew you fell and all, but before that. I felt something—gnawing at me. I've felt it ever since I left, only... it's been getting worse."

Mrs. Henley ran a hand over the piano, petting it with soft, gentle strokes. "It was Walter's, you know. My late husband. When we first bought this house, he was so excited to have guests over. To entertain and serve drinks and laugh and tell jokes like his father used to. Well, he went out and bought this right away. He could play by ear and was so wonderful at it.

"It was in the living room back then, and I would prop my elbows up on the edge and watch Walter play. And when you played, I saw him come and sit beside you. He smiled at me like he used to as he played that very same song, and suddenly, we were young again... and together." She sniffled and squeezed an arm around my shoulder.

"I remember it differently. Something came behind me. It told me to play... to feed it my emotions. My pain."

Mrs. Henley smiled. "Music does that, doesn't it? Turns emotion into beauty. Walter used to say that if you don't feed something to the darkness, eventually, it will feed on you. And sometimes, in art, one person's tragedy is another's rapture."

"But what you saw—"

"What I saw... was a miracle. And you helped give that to me. Tell me, how did you feel afterward?"

"Free," I said without a second thought. "Free of the bad memories that were haunting me for far too long. Like suddenly, they weren't too heavy, and I could just let them go, if that makes sense. But they came back, slowly, and that's why I returned here. It was all I could think about."

She nodded. "Bad memories are like weeds. You can pull them out, but sooner or later, they sprout back, and you'll just have to deal with them all over again." She sighed and ran her fingers over the piano. "When you get to my age, all you have left are memories. Good, bad, it doesn't make a difference. You just want to get lost in them either way."

I placed my hand over hers and squeezed it. She was ice cold.

She snapped up the keyboard cover and turned toward me. "I'm tired of running from them. Will you play for me? Just one more time?"

I nodded.

Again, I felt the magnetic pull at my hands. The keys were so cold, begging for me to touch them. I cracked my knuckles and placed my fingers in position. They rolled over the keys, letting the sound twinkle across the keys.

The wind whipped up around me. Again, I felt something at my back.

Play for me, baby.

Mrs. Henley's smile emanated from a softened face. She watched me fervently, hanging on every note.

The song was different from before. Slower. A soft breath on the nape of a neck. My fingers moved so easily, working a song only they knew.

The wind pulled harder, and the darkness pressed in. *Play for me*, I heard. The thing behind me pressed to my back. It reached across my neck and touched my hair. I could feel its hunger. I could smell its greed.

My hands struck chords like a stuttering heartbeat. Mrs. Henley reached an arm around me, and I turned toward her. She was no longer the woman I first met. She was the girl in the photo. Smiling and happy, her lover, Walter, pressed close to her face from the darkness.

The thing behind me reached through the thin layer of bone and flesh atop my head. It snuck its icy hand into my brain and pulled out what I kept hidden. The pain, the heartache, the loneliness.

Play for me, baby, I heard, and she was there behind me. My mother. She pulled a belt tight around her arm and slapped at it.

Still, I played.

I could no longer see the keys past the blurred wetness of tears. My chest heaved as I held it back.

Play for me.

Mom punched the syringe in her arm as I played for her. She collapsed as I played for her. She died as I did absolutely nothing, but I played for her.

The thing thrummed excitedly at the memory channeling to my hands in an off-tune chorus. Still, my hands kept playing. Playing like I had when it happened.

I turned to Mrs. Henley just before the darkness swallowed her and the winds took her away. Her glowing face still smiled as it rolled into the darkness like sand from an hourglass. She was happy, however. Lost in her own memories and the beautiful tune of my sadness.

All at once, the music stopped, and the winds died. I hunched over the piano, alone, and held myself as I cried. The piano, it seemed, was satisfied.

* * *

"Ah, you must be Wesley, our pianist for the evening." The man stuck out a sturdy hand toward me.

I smiled and shook it in return. "Yes, sir. I'm a volunteer with the Senior Home Services program."

He squinted and twisted his face in recognition. "You're the one that brought us the piano in the first place, aren't you?"

"Actually, sir, it was one of our members who donated it to us after she passed away. We just thought a community home like this would be a magnificent home for it."

"Well, we're very appreciative of it. The residents are very excited about your performance. They're gathered out there for you, so whenever you're ready, go ahead."

He led me to the rec room, a large open space spotted with balding heads and silver hair. At their center was the piano, although it didn't look the same. After a fresh coat of paint, the thing gleamed as if it was brand new. It sounded better, too, after a good tuning.

All eyes turned toward me as I took my place at the seat.

My chest thrummed with excitement. Just like the last time, the bad memories had come back after a while, and I had to get rid of them—in the only way I knew how.

I looked out at the crowd around me, and I remembered Mrs. Henley, how I'd played my pain for her, and somehow, she'd seen the beauty of it. She'd seen her rapture. She'd died that night—there in her hospital bed across town—yet somehow there with me.

These people here, what would they see when I played? What memories would come for them? Good, bad, it didn't make a difference. I just wanted to get lost in them either way. I wondered if they would be lost, too. Would they smile when the darkness consumed them, like Mrs. Henley, or would they scream in terror?

I could feel the piano then, the thing inside it, staring at the wrinkled faces around me, hungry, ready to eat whatever I could feed it. I'd give them all to it gladly, just to keep the darkness inside me in some far, far away place.

If you don't feed something to the darkness, eventually, it will feed on you.

I cracked my knuckles, smiled, and let the piano take hold.

Screwed in the Head

I was getting a haircut when they found the screw in my head. The scissors scraped across its metal tip, making a metallic grinding noise that sent electric shocks through my skull right down to my teeth. The hairstylist jumped at the sound, backing away with hands raised high as if the tiny screw was holding her hostage.

I reached up and felt the hard protrusion nestled in my hair. A quarter-inch from being flush in my scalp, on the left side of my head, three inches above my ear.

Surely I would have noticed if it had been there before, right?

I tried to pull it out, but it was solid. The threads firmly twisted in tissue and bone. I leaned into my reflection to see it.

Phillips head. Stainless steel.

That evening, I took a screwdriver to it. Placing the tiny cross of its tip in the plus-shaped groove. I squeezed the acrylic grip of the handle and, *lefty-loosey*, gave it a firm twist. My vision went white with pain and my neck jerked back. I torqued harder, feeling my soft brain underneath, holding to the sinew and threads that keep it in place.

The screw broke free and twisted a quarter turn. I gasped as my vision returned, and it was easy to unscrew after that. Cranking the driver with forearm and wrist as it spoiled out—*one inch... two inches... three inches...* and finally fell free. I held up the mirror and gawked into the hole in my head. At first, only the pink and red I would have expected, but then, something black poured like molasses from the wound.

What I thought was a fluid then came to life. It stretched one ropey black tendril out of the hole and then another. Tentacles quickly took shape, probing the air around me until grasping my arm and pulling itself through the hole. It fell to the floor with a wet slap and wriggled to the darkened corner.

I jumped, panicked, and returned the screw back into its hole. Each turn of the driver was agony but I twisted it deeper. The tentacles moving at my feet were motivation enough to put it back. I could feel more, too, twisting within my head.

I tried to hide the screw after that—wearing hats or scarves or growing my hair out long. But after enough time, I began to accept it. It became a part of me—the same as an eye or ear or nose, I suppose. A part that I've come to live with, serving a purpose as important as any organ I couldn't spare. So now, I wear the screw with pride.

People often look at it. I catch them when I turn too fast and see the silver gleam of its head in their eyes. They squint and smile and pretend it isn't there, all the while I can read the confusion, *the terror*, on their faces.

They're afraid of it.

Afraid of what's underneath that screw.

Yet some reach out towards it. They want to untwist the screw. To see the horrors that leak out and coil themselves around their feet.

So I let them.

Twitching with a terrified excitement, they turn the screw. The blackened tentacles reach out, slithering their long arms into eyes, and ears, and nostrils. Dark feelers take purchase, growing larger with each dizzying rush of adrenalin. Inside they scream, then they laugh. And we all feel alive as they squirm beneath the flesh.

We'll pass one another on the streets much later. They'll flash a knowing little smile and I will nod in return, because we know what twisting darkness lurks behind our eyes. We can feel it writhing within; waiting for a chance to burst free from the bone and flesh that holds it. And just maybe, one day, they'll reach up and find a screw of their own, just waiting to be loosened.

Color Me Gray

"I just want to see what it looks like," said Amber, scraping the chocolate-colored soil away from the hole. Her friends recoiled further behind her with each stony handful. Amber didn't understand their sudden disgust. Sleepovers were supposed to be fun. They were supposed to do crazy things like this. Things that would bond them together like sisters. Things they would laugh about later, give knowing looks to one another during the big soccer game in a few days. All of them bonded together, reading the other's thoughts, like high-school girls in the movies.

Instead, their lips curled back in revulsion.

Amber brushed away their looks along with the last crumbs of dirt from the lid of the weathered shoebox below her. Even with the other's reluctance, she felt her heart thrum with excitement. It was hers, after all. Lying forgotten for all these years. Left for time and the elements to do what they would with it. But what did it look like now?

The thought had plagued her since she'd buried it. She always wondered about death more than the other girls. Especially Casey, whose verbal jabs were not missed by Amber throughout the evening. Even now, among the gasps of the others, as Amber raised the box from its hole, she heard the word *psycho* hiss from Casey's perfectly plump lips.

Still, they watched.

They protested, scowled, and groaned, but they all stayed, watching over her shoulder because they refused to admit they wanted to see it too. They played like she was the psycho, but why did they all stay to watch her dig it up? Why did they stand with their arms crossed, waiting for her to finish? They felt it too. The same anticipation, the same surge of adrenalin, the same jolt of excitement. Perhaps they would still bond over this — feeling alive by looking at death.

Amber turned, box in hand, and the others stepped back as one. Cradling the box like a child, she ran her fingers over the lid, feeling the waterlogged warping of its surface. Fingers rasping across the peeling paper. Memories of the time she'd buried it rushing back.

Someone shrieked as she pulled off the lid. Amber couldn't know who because she refused to peel her eyes away.

There it was...

What was left of her old pet. Although, pet was a strong word. A lizard, more specifically a chameleon, is hardly a pet. It couldn't play fetch, couldn't run to the door when you got home, couldn't really do much more than look cool. Still, she loved it all the same. They were more like accessories, however, and in fact, people had once worn chameleons as live, colorful brooches in the late 1800s. But looking down into the box, at her dead lizard inside, there was nothing colorful about it. Only shriveled gray skin pulled tight over tiny bones.

Amber shook the box, feeling underwhelmed by what remained of her old friend. No rot, no decay, no maggots. Nothing to gawk at, nothing to induce the screams, the hurried heartbeats. Nothing of the bonding experience it was supposed to be.

"I'm calling my mom and going home," Casey said, turning her back and unlocking the bedazzled phone from her back pocket.

"Wait," Amber said, moving toward her.

But as usual, the others followed Casey like her neon pink shadow, enveloping her in their cocoon. All of them walked away, abandoning the slumber party, abandoning Amber, alone with a dead lizard still in hand.

The words *weird* and *gross* cut through their whispers. Hushed judgments that would bring them together—against her. One by one, they all left until Amber carried the box to her room. A room that should have been bursting with gossip and nail polish. Instead, Amber placed the box in her closet and sat on the bed, feeling like the psycho they'd all made her out to be.

* * *

The night was a restless one. Aside from the late hours and tears shed over what should have been, Amber was plagued by dreams of dry, gray skin. The creature, she dreamed, crawled from her closet in the night, creeping over her motionless body, dragging its tail like sandpaper over her legs. Feeling its split hands, pinching her soft flesh as it wobbled its way forward, moving for her ear like an alien lover.

It will whisper, she thought as it crawled closer. Its eyes flicked to her quivering lips one at a time. Still, she remained motionless—somehow knowing it was a dream. Knowing she could stop it at any moment.

It moved closer, nuzzling against her side, grating her cheek with its cracked skin. She held her breath, waiting for its elastic tongue to worm its way across her or slip into her ear. Instead, it hissed while resting on her shoulder just like it had when it was alive so long ago—when she was young.

She could hear it. Faint wheezing breaths against her ear. Warm breath that smelled of mold and fermented fruit. Breath that shouldn't have been because it was dead. Each exhale landed in her ear before dancing across the crook of her neck. The foul air raised tiny hairs and goose pimples along her skin.

Amber twitched, listening to the crackle of its smacking lips.

She turned to face it. To see its torn gray flesh. To see its open mouth.

Then, it moaned. A croaking sound that rose from a dull whine into a sound that was all too familiar. A word.

Amber...

She opened her mouth and gasped, forcing her eyes open to the gloomy morning light filtering in through the window.

Nothing but nightmares.

It all compounded into an ache growing in her bones. A restless night's sleep brought on by sadness and bad dreams—a feeling she struggled to shake from her head. Each time she tried, the memories of her childhood came rushing back. The loneliness and isolation she'd felt. How her old pet had helped take that away.

It was always hard making friends. She was different from other girls, and people didn't like *different*. She'd always begged her mom and dad for a sister when she was young; just to have someone to play with. Someone who would never leave her side or judge her for being different.

Instead, she'd got a pet. But not a cat or dog since Mom was allergic. A lizard. It was fitting in a way, having a chameleon as a pet. Like her, it was different. Like her, it changed itself to blend in with its surroundings. This was what drew her to it as a child. He would sit on her shoulder while Amber stroked the bump on his head, and the loneliness and isolation drifted away. They were different, together.

But now it was gone. Gone like her so-called friends that had abandoned her the previous night. Worse yet, she still had to play soccer with them. All while dead tired thanks to the nightmare, searching for energy that wasn't there.

The upcoming game was the biggest one yet, and their coach had them practicing twice as hard. He had been drilling them relentlessly for weeks, leaning on Casey's shocking ability to find the back of the net in every game.

Casey...

She was already on the field when Amber arrived. Strutting in seemingly new cleats. Bouncing a perfect ponytail that flowed like a horse's mane. How she always did so well, with so little effort, was beyond Amber. Amber had always been the one that had to put in the most effort. The time and dedication needed to excel, and still, Casey bested her without batting an eye. All without breaking a sweat that would threaten to ruin her carefully applied makeup.

Nevertheless, they had been friends growing up which made last night sting even worse. They were drifting apart, and last night had severed what was left of the thread that still connected them.

Amber jogged toward the gaggle of girls surrounding Casey, ready to apologize, move on, and save what was left of their friendship. But as Casey's almond-shaped eyes turned toward her, she watched Casey's bottom lip flick the word off her two front teeth.

Freak...

Laughter followed. Laughter at her expense. Mouths snickering behind open hands, eyes all looking in her direction.

Amber shriveled, shrinking like dried flesh. *She* was the freak? This couldn't be right. She remembered how Casey barricaded herself in a closet until her parents bought her the new phone she wanted. She remembered when Casey spit in Devon's food every day for a week, just so she could laugh as he ate it. She remembered how Casey made up allegations to get Mr. Hartwood fired for giving her a bad grade. She was not the freak—*Casey* was.

Amber strode right to her, watching the other girls choke down their laughter and step away, afraid they might catch something.

"Hey, Amber. We were just talking about you," Casey said, flashing her patented smile.

Amber didn't speak. Instead, she answered with a stiff shove to Casey's chest. The blow sent her reeling back like a ragdoll, feet flailing up as she thudded back to the grass.

"What's your problem?" Casey asked, kicking her cleats into Amber's knee as she stepped closer.

Hot white pain jolted through Amber. She clenched her hand into a fist and brought it down into Casey's gut. She raised it again, ready to deliver another blow to her pretty face when their coach's spider-like hand grabbed hold of her fist. She screamed as the coach pulled her away and stood between the two, demanding to know what was going on.

Amber turned, pounding her heels into the grass while she walked away. Looking down at the gash Casey had opened in her knee, Amber suddenly ran cold at the sight.

The blood...

The wound seeped colorless blood. Blood, which was gray. Gray like the dried flesh of a dead chameleon. Blood that crept along her flesh as the thing had in her dreams.

No one else stopped her. Either they didn't notice, or they didn't care. She moved farther away as a whistle blared behind her. She dipped a finger into the gray rivulets running down her leg and spread the inky fluid between her fingers. The dark color trickled down her hand.

Red was the first color taken.

* * *

The girl in the mirror was not the one Amber remembered. Her usual mauve lips were sullen and dark, flaking away like ash from a cigarette. She chewed them, attempting to bite off the color, peel back the layer of rotten flesh to reveal the floral pallet her mother had blessed her with underneath.

However, only dull gray chapped skin remained.

Panic began to rise inside her throat. She fumbled around the space, wrapped a washcloth around her finger, and dragged it across her bottom lip. Back and forth, pressing harder with each pass, trying to wipe away the stain, wearing away the skin until tears welled in her eyes. It wouldn't come off. Instead, splits ran through the dry flakes, cracking at the edges, dripping more blood from beneath.

Blood that was colorless.

Blood that was gray.

Blood that shouldn't have been.

Amber knew the color well but refused to believe it. How could she? It was her eyes, she tried to convince herself. Sudden color blindness brought on by... stress? She searched for an answer, a sane answer, but the awful truth hiding in her closet kept popping up instead. They must be related.

Her feet went thudding up the stairs before she could stop them. Pulling her to the bedroom. Pointing her to the closet. She stood there, watching the door that seemed to move with her pulse, pulling her away from the outside world with each hurried thought. It had to be connected, she thought, staring at its handle.

She reached out to it, her hairs standing on end, her fingers curling around the brass, her ears listening to the crying from within.

Crying...

Amber stopped. Something shrieked from behind the door. Wailing like a hungry child through throaty vocal cords. Bleating a sound that shivered up her spine.

She twisted the handle.

Still, the thing wailed, howling like a siren. A wounded animal, screaming for help. A scream that pierced her eardrums like broken glass. A cry that made her stomach twist.

She pulled the door open.

It was louder now. Throat-shattering wails between gasps for air. Shrieking and shrieking. She looked down at the box, its lid knocked free, and the room began to spin.

It was too big for the box now, spilling over its edges, curled up like a fetus. Only larger.

Amber gripped the doorframe as her knees felt weak.

It raised its distended head, back convulsing with each intake of breath, and tilted back to let out its moan. Still, it cried. A shape, glistening wet, mocking humanoid features.

Amber held her hands to her ears, trying to block out its horrible cries, feeling the room spin around her.

But still, it wailed. A grotesque newborn, squirming before her, curling its tail, reaching out with split hands. Its gray skin was now mottled with red.

Red...

The color missing from herself, the color now striping this creature's belly. The same color swirling in its globelike eye, swiveling up to meet her gaze.

It looked at her. It reached for her, and it cried.

She reached for the lid and pressed it on top, tucking in the twisted tail that was struggling to slither free. The box vibrated beneath her fingers with the sound of its cries. She scooped it up, clamping the lid tight to her chest. She had to get rid of it. She had to put it back before it got worse.

The box began to rumble against her. The thing twisted inside as she sprinted down the stairs, running for the outside, running for the hole. It was a mistake, she thought, tears streaming down her cheeks. She should have left it alone. She should have tried harder not to be the freak that she was. If she had, she might've still had her friends—still had Casey—still had herself.

Amber placed the box back in its hole. Still, she heard its cries. Cries like a newborn pulled from the womb and abandoned. Muffled more and more with each handful of soil she tossed atop it, but the sound still cut through her sobs and sharp grunts of panic. Tears splashed into the soft dirt.

Her heart ached more with each layer of earth laid above it. She had done this. Brought it back from death, let it feed upon herself, feed upon her color, and now, she had to stop it.

With the last bit of dirt back in place, Amber stepped back, telling herself that everything would be fine—everything would go back to normal.

However, as she stepped inside and washed the dirt from her hands, still hearing the cries in her head, still eyeing her gray lips in the mirror, she knew this was far from the truth.

***

Green was the second color taken...

Amber pressed her face close to the locker room mirror, staring into the ashen pinpricks where emeralds had once lived. Green eyes like her father's. Green like a summer forest, springing with life in the warm sun. Not now. They were pallid and colorless, and the surrounding skin stretched tight over them, growing toward the pupillary center. A forest of charred irises, burned to charcoal. Lifeless.

Amber gaped at herself, feeling stunned, not as much by the alien eyes staring back at her, but from what her coach had told her only moments earlier.

"I can't have you play in the game today," Coach said, looking down to avoid her eyes. "I've never had an issue with you before, but now... You've changed, Amber."

Her back hunched at the words.

"The team is afraid to play with you now. After what happened with Casey—"

"I'm the second-best scorer on the team," Amber said, taking a tottering step forward.

"Well... that's just it, Amber. You're the second-best, and Casey is the top scorer. Casey won't play if you are on the team. She's afraid of you—you attacked her, and frankly, you'll be lucky if she doesn't press charges. I can't let this go unanswered."

Amber had practically seen the strings tied to him. Strings pulled by Casey, just like all the others she touched. Her coach was the one who was afraid, not her. Casey used that fear to her advantage.

And now, as Amber looked at her own horrifying features in the locker room mirror, playing the coach's words over in her head, the one sight more revolting than her sullen face was the sight of Casey coming into view behind her.

Casey leaned against the doorway, watching Amber through her reflection. "I just wanted to say sorry," she said, twisting the tips of her golden hair around her finger, hair that cascaded over her shoulder like a glorious waterfall. "I shouldn't have called you that, and it was wrong. I hope we can still be friends... like we used to." She smiled.

Amber still faced the mirror. She knew that smile. A smile that, despite the blinding whiteness and perfect symmetry, hid venomous fangs. Another intimidation tactic. Surely, Casey knew what the coach had just told her. Surely, she knew what she had done. Yet now, she stood in perfect posture, acting as if she was the bigger person.

Amber's right eye turned to face her. The movement, one eye moving independently, tracking to her, was enough to erase the victory from Casey's face.

"Yes, you're right," Amber said, turning her other eye to face her. "I do hope we can still be friends."

Casey stepped back toward the lockers.

"Just like we used to, right?" Amber glided toward Casey, shaking with anticipation. "Do you remember when we were young? Do you remember how close we were?" The words hung in the air until Amber pressed between them.

"You've changed," Casey said, gulping down the words with a hard swallow. "You used to be cool. You used to be fun. But now... you're just weird. Now, you're just a freak!" Her breath quickened as her back pressed against the lockers behind them.

Amber licked her gray lips. Lips now splayed wide across her face, splitting at the corners, opening up far wider than any mouth should. It was all instinct now. Not the straight-A brain that she used in her advanced placement classes, but a smaller one, hidden away until now. A brain acting on pure, reptilian instinct.

Her hand jutted out, grabbing hold of Casey's arm and pinching her with the tripod of fingers. "Don't you want to be my friend? Like we used to be?" Amber hissed.

Casey squirmed and twisted, jerking her arm away as Amber's open mouth snaked out its gray tongue. It lingered a moment, dripping saliva to the tiled floor before punching into the lockers above her. Casey ducked, narrowly missing the blow that dented the surface of the locker and stuck to its metal.

Amber struggled to release her tongue, pulling back until it freed with a snap and retracted back in her head. By then, Casey was already gone. And once again, Amber was alone, missing the color that used to be in her life.

***

Brown was the final color taken.

Her skin faded fast on the way home, gray sucking the caramel from her flesh like the delicious center of a candy.

Stealing the color, leaving only a hardened shell on the surface. It felt like armor, she thought, running her fingers across the bumps and calluses lining her skin.

Had she always been this way?

Amber ran her fingers across the gray spines where her brunette hair once lived. The bony protrusions made her frown. Perhaps, this had been living inside her all along, but this wasn't her. This wasn't the life she wanted. This wasn't the life she expected it to be. This was something she tried to push down. As much as she hated to admit it, Casey was right. Amber had become a shadow of her former self. A color and shape almost unrecognizable.

However, her old pet chameleon had taught her one thing: camouflage. That was how she and Casey had become friends. She would change to blend in with what was around her. She would look like all the other girls on the outside, and hopefully, they wouldn't see the horrible creature living underneath.

But now they saw. Now, they knew.

Amber's three-pronged hand grasped the rusted hammer she had found near the shed. She could stop it. Since burying it again hadn't worked, she would have to destroy it. Smash it until it splashed red on her lips. Spraying her color back to its brilliant hue. But standing over the hole, remembering the sound of its cries, she knew it wouldn't be that simple.

Just as Amber had suspected, the hole was empty. Despite everything, she had seen it. Watching her sleep at night. Standing in the shadow of her closet. The red of her lips gleaming in its eye, wearing the brown of her skin on its own, flashing the green of her eyes across its back. It was far too big to fit in the hole now.

The nightmare never stopped.

Every night, it came for her, moving in the darkness, pulsing in jerky movements.

Always watching her, always moving closer.

In the pitch of her room and the haze of her dreams, it seemed to almost look like her. Moving over the foot of her bed. A horrid reflection with an angular head. Standing just as tall, feeling just as alone, feeling just as misunderstood.

What would it hunger for next? When the last of the color—the last of Amber—was taken, and all that was left was shriveled and gray, what would come next? It was a part of her, nonetheless. A part she'd buried so long ago. The reptilian half left dormant below the surface until she had dug it up. She had fed it parts of herself. She had given in to an instinct she had tried to suppress. And now, it watched from the corners, disguised as its surroundings—disguised as her—hungry for more.

She could feel it behind her then, dressed as her, wearing her colors, mimicking her movements. Ready to step in and take her place. Ready to do what it was that she could not. Ready to paint itself in the colors of her dreams.

Amber dropped the hammer and decided that, now, she would let it.

*　*　*

Of course, they had a party to celebrate their win.

The big win that Amber should have been a part of. She watched from outside Casey's house, blending in with the darkness, blending in with the nothingness. The other girls smiled. The girls laughed. They were swirling in a storm of gossip and nail polish—all without her. They were forming the memories, the bonds that would last them a lifetime. The knowing glances, reading each other's minds like sisters, all while Amber was left out. Because she was a freak.

Because of Casey.

Amber pressed her face closer to the window, her bulging eye flicking from one girl to the next until it spotted the blonde-haired beauty. Breath fogged on the glass with each rattling exhale. She traced her fingers along the window, feeling the paint flake away under her fingertips, and twisted a fingernail underneath.

This is what has to be done, she thought. She would take Casey's color. She would make her the freak. She would make her outside match her gray inside. She would leave her as empty as her own calloused heart.

The window screamed, wood splintering as she raised it.

The girls turned to look—but they didn't see her at first. They couldn't see her. She was nothingness, just the same. Amber watched their eyes turn wide with panic as she pulled her crooked frame through the window opening.

Laughter and gossip turned to gasps and screams as Amber rose to meet them, her back hunched and her gray flesh cracking with each movement. She tasted the air, smelling their fear, salivating at their terror, but searching for their queen.

Just then, Casey caught her eye.

She was already reeling back, trembling at what had become of her old friend, at what she'd created. The freak that she had set free. This was what Casey deserved. This was what she would turn her into.

There was a glint of recognition in Casey's eyes before she turned and ran for the door, leaving her pink cocoon of girls standing between them.

Amber lowered her bulldozer of a head and plowed through them.

Casey looked back as she reached for the door, ready to run, and swung it open, ready to abandon Amber once again. But a figure stood in the opening, blocking her escape.

Still, Amber moved closer, dragging her tail along the soft pink carpet.

Casey looked up at the dark silhouette in the doorway and shook her head.

"No…" the word bled out from trembling ruby red lips as the figure stepped into the light.

A figure with smooth caramel skin. A figure with emeralds for eyes. A figure with luscious mauve lips.

Casey jerked her head between the two as they pressed in on either side. One twisted and gray, closing in from the opened window. The other young and beautiful, standing in the open doorway, wearing a twisted grin.

Casey had nowhere left to go. She stood rigid in disbelief as the two squeezed in on her like closing jaws. Their eyes narrow and tethered to hers, their mouths unhinged and wide. Each mirroring the other's movement with every lurching step.

"You know," they both said, speaking as one. "You should be careful who you call a freak." The words came from both their mouths, sounds assaulting Casey from both sides, hissing words spoken in perfect synchronicity. "Sooner or later, one of those people might just turn into one."

Casey screamed as hands clamped onto her milk-white flesh. Rubbery tongues tangled in her golden straw hair and mouths closed around her ocean blue eyes.

Amber couldn't help but smile as the red splashed onto her lips. Of all the colors, that was the one she had missed the most.

Amber stopped to wipe a dirty hand across her sweaty brow. Digging was hard work in this warm weather after all but, as she caught her breath and took in the garden around her, it was all worth the effort. Spring seemed to make everything burst with color. Plants and trees were blooming, rising to bathe in the sunlight. Even herself, she considered while looking over her soiled hands, blossoming with color once more. It was a breath of relief as pure as the cool breeze around her.

"Are you ready?" she asked, turning to the new friend beside her.

The new friend smiled before giving an assured nod. A nod that loosened strands of her golden hair, sending them fluttering in the wind.

Amber reached out to her new friend, who looked remarkably like her old friend, and took the worn shoebox from her hands. "One last look," she said, and the other giggled in agreement.

Amber pulled the lid off the box and looked longingly inside. The shriveled doll slid slightly as she shook the box, and they both marveled at its fascinating dried gray features.

"Okay," she said, replacing the lid and squatting next to the hole. "This time, I won't dig it up. Promise."

Her new friend giggled again.

With the box in its home, the two worked as one, burying it without a word. They moved the soil on top together, shooting each other knowing glances, reading each other's minds, just like sisters.

With the last handful of soil in place, the two rose and brushed the dirt from their hands. Together, they walked away, interlocking their pinkies mid-step.

"I have an idea!" Amber said, bristling with excitement. "Let's do something fun. Let's do something crazy! After all, sleepovers are supposed to be fun, you know?"

What Face Will You Wear Today?

Y ou remember distinctly the day it happened, don't you? This came out in earlier sessions, but perhaps hearing it again will help. You are so young, after all. Young enough to see the world through an orange haze of carelessness, yet old enough to remember the day with a cellular clarity. Only to repress this memory along with... *the others*, of course.

If you close your eyes, perhaps you can see it. Steam pouring from the cracked bathroom door. The static hiss of the shower drawing you closer. You grab the handle, warm and slick in your small hand, and you jar the door just enough until you see her.

Your mother.

She stands hunched over the sink with her back facing you—nude except for the towel wrapping her hair. You watch closely, following each little knob in her back as they compress and straighten, rising in the mirror before you. But in that reflection, what do you see?

Well, you see that her face... is gone.

This, perhaps, could be attributed to a child's overactive imagination, but *your* brain... is special. You see things differently than others, and what *you* see is a bone white hollow lined with her same sun-kissed flesh—tracing your mother's hairline, to her ears, to the tip of her acute chin with only emptiness between.

You jerk your hand back, but you can't look away, can you? You watch through the opening as she reaches for the far left drawer, sliding it open to reveal the face you know. She lifts it to her head and snaps it into place. Eyes move and lips flex. She presses one cheek to the mirror and then the other, inspecting the fit.

Then, her eyes lock onto you.

You run then. Sprinting through the hall, leaping into bed and tossing the covers over you. You tug at your own face, searching for a seam, or latch, or button to open it, but find none. And when Mother comes, trying to explain—to calm you—you refuse to listen. How could you? To you, this stranger looks like your mother, but isn't. This *thing* is wearing her face. Only, her whisper soft voice is exactly how you remember, isn't it? And when she strokes your back, pressing nails ever so slightly, your trembling suddenly stops. When you finally peel back the covers, you see the same honey-brown eyes you'd always known.

"There is nothing to be afraid of," she explains.

She sees your resignation. The half-squint of your eyes. The searching look.

Still, you don't speak. Instead, you watch her, imagining that empty space you'd seen only moments earlier.

"There's nothing to be afraid of. *This* is the only face you need to remember, okay? This is the face that will always love you. Forever and ever... no matter what."

She smiles and lets you touch her face with both hands, pinching rounded cheeks and tracing her ears, searching for a seam but finding none. What you saw doesn't matter then, because she *is* your mother and you can feel it in your bones. Like a newborn cub instinctively knows which teat to suckle, you can recognize her anywhere. This is the same face that smiles when she tickles your toes. The same lips that kiss the part in your hair each night. The same eyes that crease only the slightest when she says she loves you to the moon and back.

What more can you ask for in a mother's face?

Ahhh... you *do* remember this now, don't you? Yes, I can see it in your eyes. This is what you tell the first responders, and much later the doctors, while under hypnosis. How she leads you to the kitchen after that, and makes you the biggest bowl of ice cream you've ever seen, complete with chocolate syrup, sprinkles, and a heaping mound of whipped cream.

But you know the truth of it all now, don't you?

You know that this never happened, *yes*?

Good... good. It must be a hard pill to swallow, I imagine, and I don't mean because of your... *condition*.

Now, where are we? Yes, the truth of the matter.

Your father is a very ill man. And his brain is *special*, like yours. So when he sees something—something that isn't there but his brain tells him it is—he acts out on it, even though it isn't rational.

He makes you watch, doesn't he?

He makes you watch through the steam-filled bathroom and the static hiss of the water because the sound keeps the voices quiet for him. And he places the knife to her face, and he searches for a seam that isn't there. He removes her face... in front of you.

Please, I know this is hard, but it is all part of your recovery. You have to live the reality of it, not the fantasy.

You stay with her after that. You waste away for days until they find you. You're alone, and tell them your story, but they figure out what truly happened, don't they? And your father is nowhere to be found. But days later, when you see his face, when you read that bold headline above his photo on the news, what do you do?

We don't know how you found the knife. Perhaps you pocketed it from a careless employee, but even you don't know the reality of that one, yes?

We find you just in time. It's amazing how your derangement is so deep, you can almost finish removing your own face, only to pass out from blood loss before it's complete.

The surgeons try their best with you, but they can only do so much. The nerve damage and scar tissue leave you... well, let's just say, *altered*. And while it must be difficult—living this again, knowing the truth of what transpired—you know why we must go through this, yes? There are gaps in the story. Gaps only you can help us fill in. So please, whenever you're ready, pick up that pen and paper.

We would like to speak to your father... if you'd be so kind as to let him out. You know he's inside there with you, yes?

I Found It at the Record Store

I like to think I have a keen eye for rarities. Somehow, every time my fingers flick through the weathered sleeves in the back of a shop, I always find that one gem. That one overlooked record that eluded not only the eye of the store's clerk, but every other person who browsed past it.

This time was different.

I could tell it was different the moment my fingertips touched it. It just *felt* different. The paper jacket was sharp, jagged at the end. Which isn't a good sign but it did catch my attention. The plain-yellowed covering had seen better days, and those days were probably a *very* long time ago.

It practically fell from the sleeve into my hand. Running to me like it wanted me to have it. There was no label visible, no markings. I held it to the light and examined it. Slightly warped, but for its age, pretty clean. No scratches, scuffs, or skate marks, and also no track breaks in the grooves. Just one long recording. *Strange.* It was a very old, very clean, mystery record, and it was only fifty cents. Well worth it.

I went to place it back in the sleeve and that's when I noticed there was something else inside. I tilted the jacket and shook until it slid free, falling like a leaf from a tree.

A photograph.

The dated black and white picture lay face up on the floor. My heart pounded like a bass drum as I picked it up. In my years of digging, I've certainly found some strange stuff hidden in records: money, concert tickets, drugs, (I always like finding those things), but never anything like this. It was a weathered picture of a boy wearing a long forgotten style of clothes, leaning against a tombstone. His eyes were solid white in that weird way eyes looked in old photos.

I shivered at the sight.

Just an old photo, I told myself, but something about it seemed to crawl under my skin. The boy's look, the grave, the odd place I found it—it was unsettling. I mean, it could have been anyone. Maybe even my grandpa as a child, standing at someone's grave on the farm.

The farmhouse behind him did look familiar, didn't it?

It wasn't, and it didn't.

I glanced around and no one was watching, so I slipped the picture into my pocket. I tossed the record in a stack with a few more random records, and went to the register.

Fifty cents, I thought as he rang it up. A deal for any record, but what in the hell was this one?

***

Noodles came right to me when I got home. His meowing echoed in the empty place as he rubbed himself around my ankle.

"At least she didn't take you," I said, brushing the side of his cheek and scooping him up. "Or you," I said, stepping inside my vinyl stuffed den. It was all I had now, my turntables, my record collection, and my cat. My ex took a lot from me, but I would never let her take these precious things.

I put Noodles on his perch by the window and pulled the mystery record from under my arm. I looked it over again and held it up to Noodles.

"What do you think, huh? Tommy Johnson? Frank Wilson?"

He held his leg up and started licking it in that weird way cats do.

"Thanks. Real helpful."

I set the record down and removed the picture. My veins ran cold once again at the mere sight of it.

Why? What was it about *this* one that seemed so different? I turned it over. Nothing on the back. It had to be eighty, maybe ninety years old. What did that say about the record?

I set the photo on a shelf above the turntables. It felt like the boy was watching me while I held the strange record up to my eye. I flipped it over, only this time I noticed the faint 'A' scratched by hand near the spot a label would be.

I placed it on the turntable, A-side up, and flipped the knob, bringing the disc to life.

It wobbled as it spun—waving with that warping I noticed earlier. I switched to line one on the mixer, slid the fader left, and thumbed the volume to a comfortable four.

"Here we go Nood—" I looked over but he was gone. *Cats...* I thought.

I reached toward the needle, ignoring the small tremble in my hand. I've felt like this before when putting on a new record, but it was usually from excitement. Not like this. I was afraid. *Actually* afraid for some reason.

I swung the arm over as carefully as my hand would allow, and placed the needle at the record's edge.

A short thump of bass sounded as the needle touched the vinyl and bobbed with its movement. I held my breath until the pop and hiss came through the speakers. Every time I hear that sound, I feel the warm fuzz surge through me. Even then, underneath the nervousness I was buzzing with excitement. I was possibly the first person to hear this thing in almost a hundred years.

I leaned closer.

The static grew louder.

I focused my ear and slid the volume up a hair.

There was nothing, until suddenly screams erupted from the speakers.

I jumped back as the blood curdling sound continued. Harsh, painful cries rumbled across the speakers. I ripped the needle off the record, letting it squeal as I dragged it across the grooves.

"What the hell!" I recoiled away from the table as the record continued to spin. I was out of breath, ears still ringing with the sound, and I could feel my heartbeat in my throat.

I waited a moment, just watching it, trying to slow my pulse. To process what it was I heard. *The screams, the pain*, it sounded like pure torture. I've heard screaming in songs before—but this wasn't *that*. This was pain. Pure distilled suffering, carved into wax.

I approached the table as if it might reach up and grab me. Slowly, I flipped the power switch and watched the record creep to a halt. I stared at the black circle with even more questions now. I let out a flimsy breath and looked towards the picture on the shelf.

He moved.

The boy in the picture turned his lifeless eyes toward me, smiled, and then waved.

***

What was happening to me?

I paced outside the closed door to the den, too afraid to go back inside. Was I going crazy? Pictures don't move, records don't scream. I knew there was something funny about that damn record, only I didn't expect this.

I couldn't get it out of my head. The picture moved. I'd seen it before running to the bathroom and splashing water on my face. It didn't make sense. I stood at the door, convincing myself I was wrong. I had to be, because the only other explanation was... bad.

I pulled myself together and opened the door. The room looked the same. *A good sign*, I thought. I walked to the table and looked at the picture once again.

There he was, the boy. Standing in the same position and definitely *not* moving.

Okay, so maybe I'm tripping.

I looked at the record sitting on the turntable. Maybe it was laced with LSD, or released some toxin that messed with my head. The only way to find out would be to listen again. I had to see what in the hell it was. I had to know for sure.

Again, I flicked the power on and the record spun to life. I lowered the volume and then reached for the needle's arm. The record hissed with static as I lowered the needle to its edge, and I waited.

Screams rang over the fuzz once again. The sounds were just as painful. They actually hurt. Each throat-shattering scream sent a wave of torment tearing through my chest. I wanted to stop it, I wanted to rip the record off the table and break it. I reached for the record when suddenly it all went quiet. I paused, leaning in as tears filled my eyes when—

* * *

The men surround me. Their faces, hidden by the hoods of their cloaks, but I know who they are. I know what they want. They speak words I don't know. They speak in a single unified voice

Splash.

The liquid falls on me. It burns. My insides scream.

Splash.

More burning, I writhe as they watch. The thing inside grows with rage.

I don't want it here.

Their books close with a puff of dust.

It's closer now.

I see the glint of their blade.

They raise it.

I scream.

My insides scream.

Something crackles beside me.

The blade moves.

The sound grows louder.

Repeating, pushing the darkness away until I hear—

* * *

The record clicked and repeated, spinning at its end. I was on the floor of my den, sweat dripping from my face. It wasn't a dream though—I *was* there. I watched it happen *to me*. My body, the burning inside it. I placed a hand to my gut, feeling for anything stirring inside.

Nothing.

I rose to turn off the turntable and looked at the photo.

The boy was gone.

The grave, the farm—it all was all there, but the boy had disappeared. I took the picture from the shelf, watching it, waiting for something to move again.

It didn't.

But now, something was written on the other side.

166 Forest Glen

This definitely wasn't there before. I would have noticed it.

I set down the picture and wiped away tears. I had no idea what was happening, but now I knew where to look to find out.

* * *

Asking my ex to watch Noodles was a hard pill to swallow, but I had no other choice. I had to go. And after a day and a half of driving through the middle of nowhere, I ended up on the remains of a farm. The fields were swampy now, but I followed an old path through a rusted fence until it led me to a house with the same address. Windows, long since boarded over, were now tagged by some adventurous graffiti artists.

I walked around the place, pressing through the tall weeds and listening to the insect noises from inside. Sunlight filtered through the trees, as the breeze chilled the sweat clinging to my skin. Not once did I stop to think, *what am I doing?* It all seemed normal and absolutely natural. Dropping everything, driving across two states, and circling an abandoned farmhouse because I found the address on a picture that used to show a boy but he disappeared when I listened to a screaming record.

Totally. Normal.

I held out the photo and scanned the scenery, circling around to the back of the house with the picture raised, trying to line it up with the landscape. Suddenly, there it was.

The tree matched. The crumpled remains of a barn behind it matched, and sticking from the ground, right where it should be, was the tombstone.

I practically dropped the picture. I walked forward, flicking between what I saw around me, and the photo, until the scene matched up.

"This is where they took the picture," I said aloud as if the boy was listening. I expected him to be there with me.

He wasn't.

I moved forward until I stood over the grave, and kneeled to read the inscription.

May his sacrifice be our rapture.

No name, no dates, just the one ominous line. I reached down to touch it and as my fingertips brushed the stone, I felt screams erupt inside me—the same screams from the record. I jumped back and covered my ears, but still, I heard them. I could *feel* them. It was as if someone had dragged my body across the grooves of a record, and the sound reverberated from within. Visions carved into my head like a needle on wax.

Suddenly, I knew what to do.

I fell to my knees and clawed at the soil. Fingertips scraping against a stony ground. My fingers stood rigid like claws. Scratching until the top layer cleared away, and rasped across the underlying wood.

Splinters raised up like needles across the grain. I pushed the remainder of dirt aside until tracing the wooden edges. A small square with a rust-stained ring on one side. I grabbed the ring and pulled. The hinges screamed like the record as a door swung open with a shudder of air. Dirt plumed around me. I waved a hand at the cloud, choking on the dusty taste.

Grit blurred my eyes but I could see wooden steps disappearing into the darkness below the headstone. *He was down there,* I told myself. *I feel him calling; I feel his pain, even from the past.*

The light from my phone was barely enough to see by, but it was all I had. The space lit up in a faint blue glow, revealing stairs and a tunnel beyond. I put my foot on the first step and tested it with my weight.

It held my weight.

I stepped down underneath the grave, listening to the wooden groan of each board along the way.

The air was stale in my lungs. A forgotten place, refusing to succumb to time. Posts braced earthen walls, walls that could collapse at any moment. I aimed the light toward the end of the tunnel and saw the gleam of red paint in the distance.

I moved closer. Each step crunching over the pounding of my pulse. I reached the door at its end. Red paint gleamed among the gray boards—a symbol painted on its surface. Six lines that met to a point at the bottom, with an arc running through them.

I raised my hand to touch it but stopped. I couldn't know if it would be like the record or the tombstone. If touch alone would plague me with its visions. But there was no going back now. I put my hand on the wood and felt nothing, so I pushed it open.

It swung open without a sound, unveiling a room that was dark, cold, and much bigger than I would have imagined. As I walked inside, I could feel my breath reverberate off the layered brick walls. Each stone must have been hand laid, and much care was taken to keep it concealed. I scanned the blackness with the light, taking in the open space and its fetid air.

"Were you down here?" I asked, listening to my voice echo across the room. I looked at the picture, still grasped in my sweaty hand, but he still wasn't there.

I moved toward the center, letting the light trace over an oversized stone slab, and I saw him.

Bones.

That's all he was now. Bones left and forgotten. Until me—until I found him. Much like the forgotten records that everyone browsed past, not recognizing them for what they were. Until I did. I have always been the one to find the lost and forgotten. That's why he called to me. That's why I found his record.

I looked at his remains and my heart panged with sadness. Only a child, lying with hands crossed at his chest.

"They did this to you," I said. "People you knew—people you loved. They did this, and left you here."

I held up the photo and looked inside. *There he was.*

Holding the picture above his remains, the boy's image moved from behind the tree. It walked across the scenery, pausing, jumping, moving in quick jerky motions. I tried to blink away the discomfort and dropped the picture. It fluttered down to his corpse like a butterfly. My feet plodded back while I watched him move closer.

Slowly, he shifted his way toward the front of the frame, until he seemed to take up the entire image. His eyes were still white, and they never wanted to leave me.

Back pressed against a stone pillar, I watched the boy reach through and grab the edges of the frame. His gray fingers jutted from the photo, sculptures come to life, worms wriggling for a hold. They grasped the sides and pulled it wider. Stretching until his head burst through the opening.

His eyes never left me.

I was stuck to the stone, petrified by the sight before me.

The boy pulled his shoulders over the frame. Gray, sullen skin climbing into reality. Joints twisting in strange ways as his body squirmed through the window to the past. He rose above the picture and stood over his corpse.

Still, he watched me.

I wanted to run, every part of my insides telling me to get as far away from that boy—*that thing*—as quickly as I could.

But I didn't.

He lunged off the table, surging straight for me. I shriveled back and turned away—pressing my eyes shut, too afraid to watch.

"Thank you," he said in a breath-like whisper. It was soft and warm, much like the static on a record.

I lifted my eyes. He stood in front of me, wearing a smile from ear to ear below colorless eyes.

"You... you're welcome," I said.

He stepped to the stone slab and lay a hand on the bones—*his* bones. He looked at the remains with a hint of sadness but still held the smile. I moved to him, thinking to comfort him in some way, but when I stepped from the pillar, his mouth opened with a crack.

His jaw widened, distended, and he tilted up to the ceiling. Black mist escaped from the growing hole. Pouring from the bits and pieces within him as his image slowly faded into the stream. The remains before him did the same, turning black, twisting, rising into the air like burnt ash.

I watched his body, his image, his spirit, rise into the ether and fade from existence. It took only a moment before there was nothing left but a stone slab and faded photograph. I wiped the wetness from my eyes with the sleeve of my shirt. It was beautiful. I felt like I truly saved him. The thought of him, trapped in there for so many years, abandoned, forgotten, waiting for someone to help set him free, it was all so sad. Yet my heart swelled with the thought that I was able to set him free. I was able to save him, to rescue the forgotten as I've always tried to do.

"Goodbye," I said with a hand on the slab, and I turned to leave, feeling satisfied that I played my part.

***

It had been pouring rain the whole trip back, and I was just thankful to have survived the white-knuckle drive.

"Psp psp psp," I called out as I stepped inside. "Noodles! I'm back buddy."

He didn't come.

I poked my head around the bare place, but he didn't show himself.

Odd, I thought, wondering if my ex finally took him, too.

I quickly opened the door to the den and stepped inside. My records were still there. At least she didn't take them.

I relaxed only a moment before I heard the sound from the speakers. A repeating soft crackle followed by a whump—the sound of a needle riding the end of a record as it spun. I treaded to the turntable, and sure enough, there it was. The mystery record, spinning on top with the needle at its end.

The crackle, the whump, playing again, and again.

Did I leave the record on the table? I wondered for a moment. Surely I would never be so careless to leave it playing like that.

I pressed the stop button on the player and watched it wind down, staring at it. Just the sight of it was unsettling. After the whole ordeal with the boy, I thought the record would just vanish, or turn to black mist or something, but there it was.

I leaned closer.

The lines scratched on it, the 'A', wasn't there.

This was the B-side.

It struck me then that I hadn't listened to the B-side. I reached down, and carefully lifted the needle, moving the arm and, instead of placing it back on its rest, setting it at the start of the grooves.

I powered on the turntable.

Again, pops and warm static filled the room. I watched the record spin, eyeing the rise and fall of the disc, and I waited.

This time, I didn't hear the screams that I expected on the other side, but instead, it was a voice. A man's voice.

"Chosen be the one who hears the screams of the forsaken, and rises to the call of the banished. Only then will the circle be complete."

I turned the volume up, and let the chill rise up my spine.

"Let the old one call to him from the screams of beyond. Let the realm be opened to release his wrath upon us!"

"Wait... What?"

"Erknock, Frajiam, erimente!"

Thunder cracked like a whip above me.

"Just... strange timing I suppose."

"Erknock, Frajiam, erimente!"

Thunder snapped again.

I looked up to the window to see what was happening outside and was taken back by the sight of Noodles, sitting on his perch growling at me.

"Noodles?"

"Erknock, Frajiam, erimente!"

He hissed at me.

"Buddy, it's me. Don't be—" but I stopped, because when I stepped closer, I looked out to the sky outside. It was dark, with clouds swirling in the distance.

"Let him come in the form he chooses. Let him open the portal and bring forth the dominion of old. Let him come!"

Noodles swatted at me before darting away, leaving only the window and the swirling red sky outside. But what startled me most, was my own thin reflection looking back at me. My eyes were cloudy and white. They watched me through the static, and just then, my own reflection waved at me, just like the boy in the photo.

Lightning cracked again and split the sky in two, spilling black mist from the void at its center.

If my years of digging through used records have taught me anything, it's that you always listen to the B-side first. Yet as I watched the horrid creatures pour from the void in the sky, my own reflection smiled, staring back through static filled eyes. He was part of me now. No longer forgotten, no longer lost, or waiting for a collector. Now he was free. And together, we watched, and listened as the screams of beyond played a rarity of its own.

Ripples of Psychosis

I see it each evening, when the sun is swallowed by the sea and the sky is set ablaze. The ocean boils from its heat, frothing until the shadows awaken and slither into the night. Shadows rise tall as a mountain, yet fluid as the sea. They taunt me with arms that reach into the heavens and pull night down on top of us.

Then, they whisper my name.

"We have to do *something*," Castile says, pulling me back to reality. Back to the ship.

I haven't told the others yet. They wouldn't understand. They can't see how the boat's rocking on the waves is a call to the beyond. A hand waving between worlds, making each day a little longer and stretching the sea as wide as infinity. All the while, we grow hungry. We grow weak. We grow mad.

"What can we do?" Marion replies. "We have no supplies—haven't seen land in months. There is nothing left but to continue sailing west."

They look to me for assurance. "Aye," I say and turn to the hideous inkblot rising from the sea.

We are stuck here I believe. It's the only explanation as to how time has passed but has not. We sail west and yet haven't moved at all. This boat is an island in a world that has ceased to exist. We are trapped somewhere between life and death with the *things* that exist between those worlds because we once existed between those worlds. Poseidon has finally caught on to it.

"West, west, west…" Castile says, circling slender arms around him. "We are sailing to our doom. We are suffering at the wits of a madman. How long until another man falls? How long until we tear at each other's throats just to see red instead of this god-forsaken blue?"

The dark shape beyond rises into the clouds until lightning slices its black veins in two. They bleed rain on top of us. They'll bleed rain for days I can tell.

"*Red…*" Marion mumbles the word with a distant stare.

Sometimes I wonder if the others see it too. The shape moving in the distance. How it makes the waves we ride. Whitecaps high as the mast as it walks across the horizon, kicking mist into the sky and pulling haze into the edges of our sight. Or, I wonder, do they hear its voice? Calling them toward it, toward the beyond?

It calls to me then—whispering over the groan of wood beneath me and the patter of rain on the deck. I hear it whisper my name in the wind. It tells me to sail a little further—hold out a little longer—teasing me with perseverance. It tells me of its warm embrace. How it will lead us to its world of obsidian and night, where the stars move in reverse and the moon is only an anchor to hold us.

I want to go.

Castile steps backward and presses himself to the rail. Light cuts through suddenly, and the gray deck turns warm as caramel. He scans the faces around him, seeing our gaunt faces as they truly are—bushy beards below haunted eyes, stained teeth and cracked skin. With each glimpse, panic rises on his own sullen face. Castile scratches at the wood behind him with a trembling hand, and then turns toward the sea below.

I stay strong for the others. I always have. I stay vigilant for the crew. They don't know what lurks on the other side. They don't see past the horizon as I do.

The ship shifts starboard as Castile splashes into the sea. It's as if it knew. As if, without him, the load is suddenly light enough to float us across the sky into the beyond.

Darkness comes as the figure approaches. Rising above the surface and casting us in its shadow. I can feel it breathing on the nape of my neck. I can hear it speak. I can hear its call.

My hands tremble on the wheel.

Just a little further. Another day, or two, or ten...

I blink the salt from my eyes and see the remaining crew surround me. All of them press shoulder to shoulder and circle me with boot heels clunking into the deck.

"Captain," Marion says, and I clench my fist and lock onto his empty stare. "We've seen it, Sir."

The others nod in unison.

"We hear it speak. We're... ready, Captain. It is time to heed its call."

"Aye," I say and finally release my grip on the wheel. It spins wildly and the ship rocks into a spray of mist. The men begin to sing. A chorus of throaty voices and guttural sounds. Together we dance, and spread our arms wide.

Finally, I think as the shadowy figure pulls us into its embrace. Finally, we are home.

On a Sea of Shadows

Vaughn watched the red string of saliva stretch from the corner of the man's mouth. It extended down, threatening to splash the tops of his polished black boots.

"They'll come," the man said, blood vessels bursting around his corneas, painting the whites of his eyes red. "They will want it, and they will come. Just like we did. Just like you are doing now... there's no way to stop it."

Vaughn's crew silenced him with another blow to his gut.

"Who?" Vaughn asked, sliding his boot back and watching the bloody globule fall to the deck.

The man grinned through blood-soaked teeth. "You don't understand what you're doing, do you? You know one thing, to take. You take lives, belongings, dreams—but you have no fucking clue what you're doing here." He spat at the man before him, and this time the blood-saliva mixture splattered Vaughn's boot.

Vaughn looked down, considering the words a moment, staring at the stain running across his foot. This had to be a first for him. No one would dare say such things to him, especially while surrounded by certain death. Did this man not know who they were? Did he not know why they were here? Surely, he knew. Surely, he accepted his fate. So why then, would he bother ruining such finely crafted footwear?

Vaughn removed his pistol and pressed it into the man's chest. Then he pulled the trigger. The weapon rang out with a cloud of smoke and thunder, spraying the flabby man's innards out through his backside and sending his body slumping back to the deck. Vaughn closed his eyes and breathed deeply, filling his nostrils with the burnt powder still lingering around him. His chest throbbed with excitement at the scent.

"Search the ship," he said, stepping wide over the man's body, avoiding the crimson fluid pooling around him. "Earn your pay, and throw this one over the rail." He dragged his boot across the dead man's shirt, trying to salvage what was left of the handcrafted leather.

Throaty voices and steel erupted across the vessel. Men finally let off their leash after many tedious days searching the sea, now perhaps even more bloodthirsty than their captain. Vaughn stepped across the planks, rising and falling with the sea like an apparition. Sliding into his place at the bow without a sound, he gripped hold of a line and stuck his face in the wind. The vessel rolled, waves slapped against the hull, and Vaughn stroked each spray of mist into his flawlessly shaped beard.

He could sense his own ship, the aptly named *Shadow*, standing behind him like its namesake. It loomed over the smaller vessel, casting it in darkness with its black flag fluttering high above. Vaughn closed his eyes, listening to the sea, soaking in the sounds of the havoc around him. The screams carried across the wind, the dull whack of steel on flesh, the churning of the ocean; it was a symphony of euphoria to his ears. An orchestra of darkness playing just for him. Death rang its melody, taking the light, leaving only darkness in his wake. Standing on the bow, overlooking the sea, Vaughn smiled to the sound of its song as only a conductor could.

Until he heard the laughter.

A dry, painful laugh, one that echoed like gunfire. One that disrupted his song, stealing the moment, stealing *his* moment, away from him. He turned and followed the noise, anger rising like the tide within him, surging with each step. He followed it until he spotted the defunct instrument. A man, almost unrecognizable among the pile of knotted ropes, bleating laughter between fits of coughs.

Vaughn walked closer to the man, striking the boards with his defined boot-heel with each step. The man's tan skin was pulled tight over atrophied muscles—no more than a pile of sinew and bone. Still, he laughed in chest-heaving bursts, each sound pulling Vaughn further from the music, further from the moment.

Vaughn stopped only paces away, eyeing the ropes cutting into the prisoner's skin, his cracked lips, his wiry neck, flexing with effort as he tried to speak.

"Fate..." he said, stretching the word until it turned into another rasping cough. "Fate has a sense of humor, it seems.

Pushing pieces across the board, only to laugh as they fall from the table." The man's voice drifted like fog, speaking with the cadence of a drunk or a madman.

Vaughn slid the cutlass from his side, using its point to lift the brim of the man's hat and reveal his chiseled face. Despite the hard lines carved across it, it was a face young and manicured. It was a face both beautiful and menacing, a face used to lure its prey before exposing pointed fangs.

"You think it is *fate* that sent me here?" Vaughn asked, squatting down to face him.

"Oh yes, I do! Although, you don't know it yet. You don't even know why you're here." He laughed again. "Do you know who that man was, the one you just killed? Do you have any idea what lives inside this ship? What we were doing here? Do you even know what it is that you're after?" The weathered man smiled, revealing blackened teeth.

Vaughn leered closer, squeezing the handle of his blade. He had killed men for less, for no reason other than the pure thrill of it at times, and had done so only moments earlier on this very ship, yet now he hesitated. Why? He considered his reluctance, stroking his beard once again, smelling the scented oil inside. Something about the man's words, the cadence of his voice, the circumstances of their arrival. It all stirred in his mind like waves on the sea, crashing and churning on the surface, only to leave him feeling seasick.

Vaughn eyed the man over, searching for the best place to slice him open, when the hurried footsteps of his men followed up the boards behind him.

"Sir," his deckhand said, pulling Vaughn away from his red thoughts. "There's nothing here, sir. Nothing on the whole damn ship! We've turned it over twice, sir, but there's nothing worth more than the wood she's made of!"

"What?" Vaughn said, pulling away, turning toward his crew. "Impossible! We were told—"

"We were told wrong, sir..."

Rage flared up inside Vaughn. His confidant had never let him down. His tips had made the captain into what he was. He was the one man Vaughn trusted, and was paid well for that trust too. Vaughn raised the edge of his blade to his deckhand's throat in one swift move. "Watch your tongue or I will remove it myself!"

The man swallowed, the hairs on his neck scraping at the sword's sharpened edge. "Aye, sir," he said, lifting on his toes to avoid the blade.

Laughter sounded again behind them.

"I told you," said the prisoner, "you don't know why you're here!"

Vaughn pulled the cutlass away and swung it round, pointing it at the prisoner. "Get him! He knows something. He knows what's here, and he's going to show us where to find it."

Vaughn brought down his cutlass with a solid chop, splitting through the ropes that bound the prisoner. The crew grabbed hold of the man while Vaughn picked stray lint from his brass-buttoned coat. All the while the words still swam in his mind. Words that were true.

You don't know why you're here.

***

The prisoner led them down a cramped set of stairs behind a galley that smelled of mold and rotted wood. With each step, they moved deeper into the belly of the ship. Twice the prisoner collapsed on shaky legs, only for Vaughn's men to catch him and prop him back up.

"This way," he said, pointing a bony finger further into the darkness. They dragged him along like a burlap sack, protesting along the way, not for his weight but for wanting to slit the man's throat instead. The storage hull was as dark as it was silent. Only slivers of light poured in from the gaps in the wood. They beamed across the space, revealing the crates and barrels now empty, upturned, or broken by the force of Vaughn's men let loose from their cage.

"There's nothing here," one of the men whispered. "We've checked this twice already."

Vaughn wondered why he'd whispered, but he felt it too. It was as if talking would disturb their surroundings.

The prisoner smiled. Even in the darkness, his black teeth gleamed like Vaughn's polished boots. "There," he said, pointing his gnarled finger to the floor. "The boards. Check under them."

The crew looked to Vaughn, who with a brief head nod sent the men forward. They traced their fingers along the edges, until they found the boards with nothing holding them. One at a time, the men pulled the planks aside, revealing the black opening underneath.

Others leaned forward, gathering around to stare into the black void below them, listening to the ship groan as it rolled with the sea. *This is no normal hole*, Vaughn thought, staring into its emptiness. It was a door. An opening into an eternity of nothingness. A world devoid of light. A space that bled darkness—thick, inky blackness. They all watched, straining to hear Vaughn's order over the pounding of their hearts.

"Ladder," he said, pointing at two men who quickly hurried away.

The prisoner didn't speak. He watched with wide pupils and a slack jaw as the men brought forward a rope ladder, fixed it to the floor, then kicked it forward into the black opening. The group stood gawking into the empty space—waiting for it to move.

Vaughn couldn't help but imagine something climbing up that ladder—something birthed from the hidden world, something eager to be let out. Vaughn closed his eyes, and listened.

It was there... whatever it was. Vaughn could feel it, moving inside, breathing beneath his feet, calling to him from beyond.

"What are you waiting for?" he said, pointing to the tallest of his men, a bald man as thin and long as a ship's mast. Vaughn gestured to the opening.

The man shifted nervously, blinking away the sweat beading on his face. He stepped to the hole's edge and looked around the room with anxious energy. None could hide their expressions, Vaughn included. They watched him like a man about to be thrown to the sea, sentenced to a fate worse than death. However, someone had to do it, and Vaughn wanted to watch.

The tall sailor dragged a soiled hand across his face and sat at the hole's edge. He swung his long legs over the dark opening and placed them inside. He exhaled between his pursed lips, and wiggled his toes to see if they still worked. "Lantern," he said, frantically motioning for a light. The crew produced one from above deck and held it out, standing as far away as possible. His long arm reached toward it before stopping midway.

His eyes twitched, blinking in surprise, sending sweat rolling down his cheeks. He looked down, staring into the opening, and gasped.

Something yanked him down, pulling at his legs with enough force to send his head reeling back, thumping onto the surrounding wood.

The men jumped at the sudden burst, struggling to react fast enough. One moment he was there, and the next he was gone, disappeared, consumed by the void. Vaughn leaned forward as a scream rang out from below—sounding from a hollow space so very far away. A sound choked on the weight of the darkness, turning his shriek to a muffled whine.

The others pressed closer, stopping at the edge, leaning over to look inside.

Nothing.

Other than the thick endless gloom, they couldn't see a thing. They turned to Vaughn, waiting for his order.

Vaughn was flush with excitement. The weight of the darkness pressed against him, whispering its secrets in a strange tongue.

Two hands ripped up from the dark opening, gripping the edge of the hole, sending the others jumping back.

The prisoner laughed.

The hands pulled, nails sinking into the wood, shaking with effort. The top of a bald head pulled up from the emptiness into the dim light.

His face held a look of frozen terror unlike anything they had ever seen. The other sailors quickly grabbed hold of his forearms and heaved upward. Pain spilled from his lips. Each pull elicited another shrill cry between his choking breaths. As hard as the men pulled, they couldn't lift him more than an inch.

The darkness below pulled harder.

Vaughn was captivated. He was almost salivating at the thought of this thing, the darkness, living inside. He knew then why he'd come here, what he'd been searching for. It was clear what he must do.

The tall man screamed as the horrifying tug-of-war threatened to rip him in two, or bring the others down with him. Screams turned to unrecognizable noise, guttural sounds of pain.

Vaughn stepped closer, smiling at the terror, watching his crew heave on the man's arms as darkness poured out around him.

Black tendrils snaked up around them. Barbs reached out for their prey, wrapping themselves around the screaming man's arms. He gasped, jerked, trying to free himself while the vines sank deeper into his flesh. The corners filled with night as light drained from the small space. Another cry of pain erupted; the barbs sank deeper, cutting into his flesh—stripping skin from bone, spilling blood down his arms, splashing red onto the crew fighting to save him, slickening their grasp with each drop. They squeezed harder, while the dark threads coiled tighter. Slowly, their fingers slipped away.

He stopped fighting then. He accepted his fate. With a face slackened, and body limp, the last bit of skin slipped away.

The crew broke free and fell backwards, landing on their backs. They scrambled away as the thing took the man down with it, and the room was silent once again.

Vaughn grinned. This was why he was here. The thought of all that power underneath his feet—a power that rose from a hole to nothingness. He had to have it. He had to know more.

The men worked fast after the pause, cutting the rope ladder free and covering the hole with boards once again. The empty crates and barrels, whatever was within reach, were piled on top to keep it below.

"You've made a mistake coming here, captain," the prisoner whispered into his ear. "We tried to warn you…"

Vaughn turned and grabbed the man by the throat. His eyes wild, his grin delirious. "What is it? Where did it come from, and how did it get on this ship?"

The prisoner looked deep into Vaughn's eyes, and laughed until thunder rang out from across the sea.

The men stopped, turning their heads above, listening to the familiar growl, waiting until it echoed again.

Cannon fire.

The sound was unmistakable, but it wasn't the trumpet of the *Shadow's* cannons.

Again the booming sounded, followed by the roar of destruction. The men squeezed through the narrow passage, running up to the deck as the thundering continued to pound in the distance.

Smoke billowed from the line of ships across the sea. A full naval fleet spread across the horizon, all pointed in their direction. They fired another volley, striking into the *Shadow* beside them. The ship, Vaughn's ship.

"Pull anchor!" Vaughn shouted. "Set sail!"

But his men only looked at him in confusion.

"What about the *Shadow*?" one asked.

"We have what we came for. We have what we need."

The men went to work quickly, pulling the sheet and swinging the sails as if their lives depended on it, because they did. The tiny ship was defenseless, but it was fast. Vaughn may have been mad, but as the *Shadow* continued to take cannon fire, it left them with no other option.

The sails quickly filled with wind and moved the ship swiftly over the waves. Vaughn turned east and hoped he wasn't too late. He looked to the prisoner from the helm. The weathered man clung to the rail and watched the *Shadow* fall into the sea below.

Vaughn watched too. He watched his ship take blow after blow as they sailed away. Pieces and debris flew from it like leaves from a tree in autumn. Soon, it rolled to its stern and the waves swallowed it. Vaughn watched, feeling the pain in his chest. Losing that ship hurt like the loss of a lover, but he already had what he wanted. Besides, there was no escaping the inevitable. A full naval fleet sailed in their direction and their only choice was to run, or fight. But they had something the others didn't.

A ship with something living in its belly.

Vaughn stepped down and paced toward the prisoner. With a forceful hand, he spun him around and threw him to the deck.

"Why are they here?" Vaughn said as he pulled his blade and held it to the man's throat. "Why aren't they shooting at us now?" His eyes were still wild, pupils as large as pieces of coal. "You will tell me what you know or I will send you under like my ship!"

The man smiled through his blackened teeth. "They've come for it too like you did. Fools just like you."

"I didn't come for that!" Even as he said it, it felt wrong.

"Except you did. Surely, you came for something. First, you heard a tale of something big being moved on a little ship. Thought it would be easy pickings. Perhaps you bit off more than you can chew."

Vaughn pulled his blade back but continued to look down at the man. "Why do they want it? What else do you know?"

"There are things in this world that very few know about. Things that hold power. And there are some out there that do know of them. Some who will stop at nothing to get them. They are drawn to it."

Vaughn knew this was true. He could feel it. The thing had a grip on him. He wanted to know its secrets—he needed to know its power. His mind opened to new, horrifying possibilities. His only limits were his imagination and his understanding.

"And how is it that you know of all this?" Vaughn squatted down and ran a gloved hand over his beard.

"I was there when we found it. The whole crew was. It consumed so many of them, ripped them to pieces... took them into darkness. Some of us tried to leave, some of us tried to stop it. It didn't work. The captain was mad with power, like you, and feared we would take it. He feared mutiny. Some were beheaded, but for some reason, I was spared. Tied up and left to die until you found me. People will come for it. They will not know why, but they are drawn to it nevertheless. Drawn to the darkness. Just like you!"

Vaughn turned his head to glare at the ships following in the distance. The words from earlier rang in his ears. *You don't know why you're here.* He wondered if the men on those distant ships knew what they were after or if they were merely pieces moved by the hand of fate as well.

"Now we're trapped with our prize," Vaughn said. "But what is it?"

"What it is, my captain... is darkness. It is the shadow. It is the evil that lives inside you. That is why you were drawn here. You are a part of it. You have lived in the shadows your whole life."

Vaughn stood and walked toward the helm. He felt it then, inside the ship, calling to him. He could sense its hunger.

"Take him into the hull and feed him to that thing. He is of no use to us now, and I want that thing kept alive!"

Vaughn looked into the wind and waited. Expecting the music, he listened for the man's scream, his shout, the one that customarily came from one sent to their death. Instead, he heard laughter. The same heaving laugh that had found him earlier. And just as before, it stole his moment, and sent a cold shiver up his spine.

* * *

The deckhands carried the captive man into the hull as he laughed along the way. The precariously stacked objects remained on top of the hidden door. As the crew stood in the dark space watching one another, they waited to see who would be the first to make a move.

"Well, it's not going to move its bloody self, is it?" said the prisoner, flashing his blackened smile.

One of the three men shoved him to the floor and started moving the objects, driven more by embarrassment than anything else. The other two followed suit, carefully moving things aside one at a time, never taking their eyes off the false boards in the floor. When the floor was bare however, all of them hesitated to move the boards aside.

"You," said one of them, "go move the boards." He waved at the prisoner lying on the floor.

Their captive chuckled. "What's wrong? Are you too scared to do it yourself?"

The man gave him a swift kick to the ribs before dragging him to his feet. "I said do it!"

With another shove, the prisoner fell toward the false door. He held his frail hands over the boards. Vaughn's men slid backward toward the stairs as his long fingers traced the boards' edges.

"Go on, open it!" one of them yelled.

The man worked the edge free with considerable effort and slid the boards aside. The darkness below sucked the remaining light from the room. An impenetrable blackness waiting to devour the light.

The prisoner looked up at the deckhands as he sat hunched over the hole. One of the crew took a careful step forward, ready to knock the man inside, but instead, black tendrils whipped from the dark hole and wrapped around the prisoner's torso. He gasped, readying a scream, but only a hiss of air came out. The three crewmates stood pressed to the wall, watching the black vine grip tighter and the color fade from the man's face.

More ropey threads rose from the hole below. They swiveled, moving closer until they converged into a single shape. A creature made of shimmering darkness stood in its place. It swung its long limbs around the horrified man. It pulled him close, casting him into the shadows, and chasing away the light. They felt it holding them in place with its gaze, stunning its prey before wrapping them in its barbs.

Voices screamed from the nothingness that enveloped them, snuffing out their cries with arms of eternal night.

* * *

Vaughn kept the vessel moving due east. Even with strong winds, the fleet ships continued to close in. He measured the distance with a raised fist, watching them encroach closer with each passing hour.

"What are we going to do when they arrive?" his deckhand asked. "We can't outfight them." His men surrounded the helm, each one wearing a mask of mutiny.

"We will outpace them, and this is not up for discussion!" Vaughn said.

"We're not outpacing anyone in this ship, sir! They're closing in. At this rate, they'll be on top of us before the night."

Vaughn did not respond. He only raised a fist to check the distance again.

His men continued. "Some are starting to worry about what we'll do when they do arrive."

"Not to mention that... thing onboard," another added. "Hanging over our heads—ready to snap our necks like the gallows rope!"

The crowd mumbled in agreement. "He's right. Men are missing. Either they jumped ship or that monster got them!"

Vaughn fixed a hard stare on his men before raising his voice. "We have no choice but to press on!"

"We do have a choice!" someone said. "We can give them what they want. We can give them that... thing!"

Vaughn saw red. It was no doubt what they were after, but the thought of giving it to them, after it had called him there, was the most absurd thing imaginable. The thing had chosen *him*. It brought him there to find it—to use it. It was something special; something powerful. Even if he did not understand it, Vaughn could never hand it over. It was, Vaughn determined, exactly what he had been searching for his whole life—only he hadn't known it until then.

He would never allow them to have it but at the same time, he would also never allow a mutiny. Vaughn had a plan to stop it all, and stop it immediately.

"Keep us on course," Vaughn barked as he stepped away from the helm. He glanced back at their anger-ridden faces. None followed as he headed below deck.

***

Vaughn wasn't sure how he would use it, yet he was certain once he saw it again, he would know. Then, it would *tell* him. The monster had called to him after all; it had brought him here in a journey that had lasted his entire life. The darkness not only lived inside him, it lived in the ship as well. It reached out to him, reached through him.

He rounded the narrow stairs, descending into the hull. The once-dark room was now spotted with light. A lantern lying on its side near the opening bathed the room in an amber glow that moved as it rolled with the rocking ship.

Vaughn grew more angry than terrified at the sight of the uncovered hole. The unattended opening meant either someone had left the hole open, or the thing had gotten out on its own. His eyes shifted over the room, searching corners for darkness as he paced toward the hole and peered inside.

The darkness was gone.

The space was no bigger than a cupboard.

Vaughn stood there, attempting to process what had happened. It was somewhere, loose on the ship. The boat shifted as a wave slammed into its side. A second wave hit and sent the ship rocking violently, threatening to capsize the small boat. Vaughn took one last look at the space where the darkness had been and staggered up the swaying staircase.

***

A wave crested over the top of the rail as Vaughn stepped onto the deck. He steadied himself and squinted into the graying sky. The fleet vessels were on top of them, slowly surrounding the tiny ship, boxing them in.

Another wave rocked the boat, sending a torrent of water over the rail and slamming into Vaughn. The blast of frigid water swept his feet out from beneath him and flung him to the boards. Another sway of the ship sent him sliding across the slick wood of the deck. The feared pirate Vaughn collapsed into a heap as his body crashed into the mast.

Pain jolted hot and white through his back from the blow as he curled around the soaked wood. He looked up to the empty helm and watched the wheel spin freely. Another glance across the deck revealed the darkness at the boat's bow.

The creature stood among the crashing waves in a shroud of black mist. Two eyes burned in its form of infinity, devoid of color. Only darkness and shadow—the very same darkness that called to him.

Its black tendrils spread from its center like a spider's web. Each thread drilled into the back of a crew member's head, Vaughn's sailors wrapped in the menacing barbs. The crew was held tethered to it, tendrils cutting deep into their flesh, draining their color. Gray, cloudy skin dripped colorless blood. Vaughn stood, steadying himself as the creature moved his men like marionettes on blackened strings.

Its eyes burned directly onto Vaughn, holding him, sensing his darkness inside. A darkness that coursed through his veins like the creature's black threads, reaching to drain the color from anything it touched. The darkness felt for another—yearning for its brethren.

Shouting came across the wind. The naval fleet was preparing to board Vaughn's ship, preparing to take what was rightfully his.

He staggered forward, toward the shadow.

The eyes of his tethered crew opened, burning white with a crackling energy.

Vaughn stepped closer, and their bodies twitched and jerked to face him.

"I am here!" Vaughn cried over the roaring wind and waves. "I am a part of you!"

The dark creature rose up, opening like a black hole, pulling in anything in its path.

Hooks clattered against the ship, grabbing onto the rail. The naval fleet hung onto the ropes.

"We will stop them! We will paint the world in darkness... together! If you show me how!"

The creature moved closer, drifting over the ship like a storm cloud.

Boots thudded twice on the deck; a sound that signaled the men boarding his ship.

The creature grew larger, stretching the void of nothingness as it drew Vaughn to its center.

"I give myself to you," he said as the color drained from his form. A black tendril whipped out, wrapping itself around his neck. "I know exactly why you sent for me," he managed to gasp.

Vaughn smiled as the black arms pulled him close, pulling him into oblivion.

* * *

The uniformed men sat around an upturned crate, watching the bound prisoner, listening with fervent attention. One man took a drink from his mug while the others remained slack-jawed.

"What happened next?" one of them said.

Their prisoner smiled, revealing stained black teeth. He was hardly more than skin and bones when they found him—tied up and bound to the mast of an empty ship. The men they were after, the pirate Vaughn and his crew, were gone. They'd wondered if the pirates had sunk along with their ship, but Captain Edwards claimed to have spied them on board the smaller ship. He declared the bound man was some sort of trap set by the thieves, and having no other option, brought him aboard the capitol ship for questioning.

"Well, what happened next?" another sailor asked the bound man, eagerly awaiting the end of the tale.

The prisoner let out a dry, painful laugh that echoed around the men like thunder.

"Well," he said, fixing a hard stare on the group, "then you brought me here... where I'll kill every last one of you, and take your ship."

His eyes went blank.

The fattest of the men let out a single huff. "You? A worthless bag of bones—tied up and surrounded by six men?" The others smiled, echoing his sentiment. "You can hardly stand, let alone sail a ship!"

"Oh, yes," said the prisoner as the shadow in the corner grew darker. The light dimmed. "That is the part that comes next, and I don't intend to do it alone..."

Their smirking faces turned white as his shadow spread across the room, growing to an all-consuming darkness. The prisoner's laughter ripped through the air like cannon fire as a dark shape coalesced behind him. Eyes burned white among a sea of inky blackness, and one by one, gray colorless shapes stepped out of the gloom. Each one tethered to the darkness with a ropey black strand. Each one with eyes burning white.

They surrounded the now petrified sailors and looked at the being at its center—a creature made of pure darkness.

"You were right," said the voice from its center, Vaughn's voice. "Fate does indeed have a sense of humor!"

Don't Eat the Candy

She tells me as we stand on the porch—*don't eat the candy.* Jess grips my arm and holds me with a piercing stare.

I nod and adjust the mask to better line up the almond eyeholes with my own. Her face is different tonight. It's not the silly pointed hat sitting above it, or the black cloak lined with a snarl of lace that wraps her—*it's her eyes.* Hard and shimmering like two polished stones.

The door flings open suddenly and a tall man wearing a wolf mask stands in the opening. "Jess," he says in the calming cadence of a therapist. "Happy Halloween. This must be the one you told me about. Come on in. Come in." He stands aside as Jess steps in, tugging at my hand to follow.

The house is casket dark and pungent like black licorice. I hear a cacophony of voices and laughter beyond the foyer, and the man in the wolf mask guides us toward the sound.

"So wonderful for you to join us," the man says, taking short, careful steps through the darkened hall. "The others will be quite thrilled to see you here."

Jess grips me tighter.

Don't eat the candy, I remember her words.

"Jess has come to every Halloween party for the last three years. It's terrific to finally meet her partner."

113

He opens the double doors ahead of me, then steps into the large room adorned with chandeliers and candlelight. Men and women cluster throughout the space, each wearing elaborate costumes and sipping from tall champagne flutes.

Jess turns to me and smiles. I smile back, but doubt she can see it under the mask.

A sound rings out, dinner chimes, and I turn to see a short man knocking a mallet against the instrument in hand. He plays it again, *high note—low note—middle note.*

The group moves to a seemingly endless mahogany table at the back of the room and seat themselves around it. I pick the seat next to Jess, three chairs from the head, and look to her for assurance. She smiles and nods, but her eyes still look like granite.

A man dressed as a revolutionary soldier stands at the head and clears his throat. "Tonight," he says in a booming voice, "is Halloween. We celebrate yet again. Another party with my distinguished friends and guests. And," his head swivels from left to right, "as with every Hallows Eve, we shall drink, and eat, and dance to celebrate life...by looking toward death."

Someone slams a fist on the table and cheers in agreement.

Jess looks at me to gauge my reaction.

Already, my pulse is racing.

"But tonight," the man at the head continues, "we have a *special* guest." He gestures a hand toward me, and all eyes follow.

The room goes silent. I can feel their gaze upon me as I look from one costumed person to the next. My heart pounds too loud—they can hear it, I know they can.

"We have a tradition here," the man continues. He hunches over the table, pressing his icy face in my direction. "The newest member *always* gets the first piece of candy."

The man in the wolf mask appears like a ship through fog. He lowers a covered platter to the table in front of me. I can see my own panic in the warped reflection of its polished silver surface. Then I see the faces, the masks, all staring at me.

Don't eat the candy.

"Only *after*," the man continues, waving his splayed fingers over the room, "will the *proper* party begin."

Wolf Mask squeezes the cover with a gloved hand, and lifts it, revealing a bone-white plate on a gleaming silver tray. At its center is a small, *harmless looking* chocolate square.

I swallow the lump in my throat and scan the surrounding faces. They lean closer, watching with hungry eyes. Waiting with eager smiles.

Don't eat the candy.

"I shouldn't," I say and turn toward Jess. Her face is impassive, and her eyes...*still hard as stone.*

"Go ahead," the man says with a smile that flickers like candlelight. "Take a bite."

My heart thumps faster. I feel my mask twitch with each hurried beat. "I don't think I—"

"Eat it!" someone yells, cutting me off.

Sweat builds behind my mask and drips hot like mercury. They lean closer, watching. Waiting. I remember what she told me, *Don't eat the candy,* but the faces around me demand it. They scream behind the eyeless holes of masks. "Eat it!" they yell, yet Jess doesn't speak.

She turns away and, in one smooth movement, I raise the candy to my mouth underneath the mask and place it on my tongue.

The room claps and howls wildly, rising to their feet in excitement.

Jess smiles but it's a smile I don't recognize.

I move my tongue left and place the candy between my teeth. I exhale a shaking breath and clench down on the piece.

Something moves inside me. It hums inside my gut, and I freeze. A sound—*a bass note*—rising through my throat and rattling inside my teeth.

The others, Jess included, move away from the table and line themselves in the center of the room. Wolf Mask grabs my chair and turns me to face them. They all watch with poised stares.

I bite again.

This time, something escapes from my lips. *More sound,* moving across my lips like a bow across tensioned strings. It vibrates the air around me with heavenly music—*high note—low note—middle note.* I stop, gasping around clenched teeth, and the sound stops, too.

The others move with the sound. One-step to the left, turning, until stopping with the silence.

I shift in my chair, feeling the sugary sweetness between my teeth, watching the mass of people frozen mid-step before me.

Wolf Mask slides his gloved hand over my face and works my jaw up and down.

The sound escapes my lips again.

Bass, violin, piano—all streaming from my mouth like a scream I cannot contain. Thumping in the rhythm of each bite. *One—two—three,* the people before me dance to its beat. They move as one. Stepping and turning with the tempo. Swinging costumed bodies with each measure, floating with the ease of marionettes.

A smile slides over my lips.

Wolf Mask disappears in the crowd as I chew faster. The music speeds up with the chewing. They all step and turn quicker. Moving through choreographed patterns as the volume builds inside my head.

Faster, louder, the song grows and builds toward a crescendo.

They flip, turn, and kick faster in a blur of movement. The sound rises until it's roaring inside my head. Screaming from within me. *High note—low note—middle note.* It becomes unbearable, screeching in my ears at a deafening volume. I can't take anymore—the sound, the ringing in my head—yet I can't stop. I grip the sides of my chair when suddenly, the song ends with a clanging splash of cymbals.

The people before me drop to the floor. They lay rag-doll limp, motionless, and though I wait, none seem to move.

I stand and step toward Jess, eyeing her dark cloak in a rumpled heap before me. I kneel to her side, but I already know something's wrong—*the smell.*

The air tastes old and fetid, filling my nostrils with its illness. I roll Jess toward me too easily, *she's too light*, and then I see her. Her skin now taut over skeletal remains. Her lips, desiccated and shriveled, curled back around exposed teeth and jaw. Where Jess just stood, only a corpse remains, wearing her clothes and staring at me from two polished stones pressed into her skull.

I peddle backward, catching a heel on another. I look down at more shriveled remains inside a costume that only moments ago held a man.

All of them... Rotten flesh and spindly bones, staring blankly from the gleaming eyes of smooth granite.

I turn and run, and try to scream, but only music pours out. Bass, strings, piano—all playing to the tune of my cries as I sprint into the night. Over the melody that escapes from my lips, I hear words hiss out from cadaverous teeth...

Don't eat the candy.

Loose Lips

Wishing someone would drown was the exact opposite of what a lifeguard should do, but as Ronnie watched the twenty-something-year-old girl smile and splash at her friends, it was exactly what she wanted. Something about this girl created an instant hatred that bubbled up inside her. It pressed on her skull, narrowing her eyes and furrowing her brow behind a brand new pair of mirrored sunglasses.

Still, Ronnie watched her, trying to pinpoint the source of her hatred. At first glance, the girl could be mistaken for a young Angelina Jolie. The same sculpted brows and bright, almond-shaped eyes. Perhaps this was what irritated Ronnie. Or it may have been the way the girl's swimsuit rode too low on her hips, accentuating each well-tanned curve. Or it could be how she twirled her chestnut brown hair around a slender finger while talking—but, no, that wasn't it either.

It was her lips.

Red and glistening like two cherry-flavored lollipops. Flawless in their symmetry, with a wave of delicate curves that met at their pinched corners. Lips that would even make Angelina jealous. They were perfect. They were hypnotizing. They were nothing like Ronnie's.

Ronnie chewed her own lip at that thought, stretching her teeth up toward the pale scar that ran across her upper lip toward her left nostril. The scar was a small price to pay from what it looked like before the surgery. Being born with a cleft lip was an injustice so cruel even Ronnie, who wished pretty girls would drown, would never wish it upon another.

And though the surgery had fixed the awful picture of who she was, the scar was still there and always would be. After all, scars were just reminders of the ugliness that once was, and Ronnie knew that more than anyone. She felt it each and every time she looked in the mirror and saw it—that ugliness. So did all the others, she thought. She could see it in the quick dart of their eyes each time she smiled, looking down at her lips and turning away in disgust.

A look this girl would never see. No, not with those two crimson beauties.

The bitch.

If those same lips fell under the water, Ronnie might not even save her. She would let those beautiful lips suck in the chlorinated water and fill her lungs with fluid instead of air until her body stopped fighting.

The pool emptied out to leave only Ronnie, the last guard on duty, and this girl, sitting on the pool's edge, swinging her toes lazily in the water.

Despite Ronnie's bitter imagination, no one had ever drowned here. Ronnie and the other guards were there for liability reasons—because the state required it. In the five years Ronnie had worked there, not one person had ever needed saving. Oh, there were plenty of whistle blows at running kids and the occasional fishing of a dead mouse out of the pool, but that was pretty much it. That and getting incredibly tan, of course. Overall, it wasn't a bad gig, in Ronnie's opinion, as long as you could get past the boring moments like these.

The sudden quiet of the place pulled heavily on her eyelids. The sun tucked itself behind the treetops, bringing a coolness that seemed to melt away muscles and stress. For a moment, Ronnie didn't even hate this pretty stranger of a girl anymore. The hollow darkness of sleep was lapping at the edges of her consciousness, and her thoughts turned cloudy as the minutes ticked by.

This girl and her perfect lips must have felt this too because she rose, wrapped a towel around her waist, and moved to recline back in one of the lounge chairs. She flashed a flawless smile at Ronnie before turning away and resting an arm above her head.

That was the last thing Ronnie remembered before nodding off to sleep.

Then, the screams woke her.

***

The police stood with thumbs in their belt, barking questions at Ronnie. Questions she should have known the answers to, but she didn't.

"So," one officer said, "you didn't see what happened? One minute, she's sitting there in front of you, and the next, she's floating face-down?"

Ronnie didn't tell them she fell asleep, she couldn't. She had one job—one fucking job—and she'd screwed it up.

"Yes." Ronnie swallowed what felt like razor blades in her throat. "Like that."

The two officers exchanged a brief glance. "Then, what happened?"

I don't know because I was asleep! I wished she would drown, and I nodded off, and she actually fucking did it!

"I heard the screaming. I jumped up to see a girl—a kid, really—staring down and screaming at the girl... floating in the water. I dove in like I trained to do a hundred times before but never actually had to..."

A sob hitched in her voice, and one man gave her a brief squeeze on her shoulder.

"The kid kept screaming, watching from the edge and screaming, and the girl didn't move. She was floating, face down."

I did this, Ronnie thought. *I killed her.*

"Was anyone else there? Do you remember seeing anyone or anything funny?"

"No," she said, and her mind went back to the pink clouds spreading from the body like reaching tendrils in the water, rolling outward and fading into the chemical-clear pool. Ronnie recognized the hair. She knew it was her. She'd wished she would drown, and it actually happened.

"What did you do next?"

"I grabbed hold of the girl. She was cold. She was still. I rolled her over, and then I saw her face. Her lips..."

Nothing could scrub the memory from her mind. How could it? Those perfect cherry pieces—gone. In their place, blood-soaked teeth now glared up at Ronnie from the ragged edges of torn-out flesh. Her lips were somehow ripped off her face. Guilt panged like a thudding drum inside Ronnie's chest. Her breathing quickened until tears ran down her cheeks.

"I think that's enough," one officer said. "Thank you."

"What happened to her?" Ronnie asked as they turned to leave. "To her lips, I mean. What happened?"

"She drowned," the officer said plainly. "Chances are she bit off her own lips while fighting for air. Trying to survive. We've seen strange things happen to drowning victims in their last moments. This is just one of the worst. It's a shame, though, that you didn't notice. You could have saved her." They gave Ronnie a disapproving stare, and their eyes flicked down to her lip—to the scar.

Every emotion welled up inside her at once, guilt, hate, fear. Ronnie had done this, and they knew it. The officers could see straight through her as if they knew what she had done. But... just *what* had she done?

"Oh, and one more thing," the other officer said, spinning back. "Would you be able to supply us with your dental records?"

"Dental records? Why?" Ronnie asked, even more confused.

"We have a body with..." he knocked his head from side to side, deciding on the proper words, "bite marks, we'll say, and no witnesses. Procedural stuff, just to be sure. I hope you understand."

"Uh, sure. But you don't actually think that I'm the one that—"

"If you think of anything else, give us a call." He held a business card toward Ronnie, who hesitated but took it from his outstretched fingers. "We'll be in touch," he said and turned to walk away.

Dental records...

Ronnie stared at the card and jammed it into the mesh pocket of her red shorts. Just *what* in the hell had happened when she fell asleep? She prodded her mind for an answer but found nothing. Nothing but a tiny voice telling her that this was all her fault. Reminding her that she was the one who'd wished for it.

***

The apartment felt colder than usual when Ronnie got home. She shivered and wrapped her arms around herself before locking the door behind her. The space, although matchbox small and in need of a fresh coat of paint, was still more than what most college students had, and Ronnie was damn proud of it. She even planned to stay after graduating next semester while finally searching for a new job. Hopefully one that didn't depend on keeping people alive.

She walked the four paces to the bathroom and ran the shower as hot as it would go. Even then, with the age of the place, it was really only slightly hotter than warm. She let the room fill with steam and leaned into her reflection in the mirror.

The image from earlier was still front and center in her thoughts. The girl and her cherry-red lips—gone. Lips the color of blood bitten off as she ferociously gasped for air. Ronnie tried to imagine what that would be like. Drowning. Sucking in water, convulsing as your lungs yearned for another breath. Reaching for someone, begging, crying for help. Then, in a flurry of panic and pain, you bite through and perhaps swallow your own two lips.

Ronnie sucked her lips in her mouth and clenched teeth around them. The scar burned pink and white in her reflection. A mountain of tissue crossing her otherwise beautiful face. She bit down hard, thinking of the girl. Squishing teeth into her own flesh, she stopped. She wanted to sink her teeth deeper but couldn't.

She'd always wanted to bite off that damned scar, ever since childhood, but her body wouldn't let her. Every time someone looked and made a face or laughed behind a cupped hand, she wished she had the strength to do it.

The officers she spoke to earlier gave her the same look, a pinched back cheek as their eyes traced the ridge of raised flesh, but there was something else in their stare as well.

Shame.

Ronnie saw it, too, while staring into the mirror. She fell asleep, wishing she had those same lips because that girl had no fucking clue how easy she had it. She saw people melt at her smile instead of wincing. She had people hang on her every word because they came from between those lips. She probably took every supple kiss for granted. Ronnie couldn't help but think of those lips pressed to her own. Wishing those lips were her own and hating this pretty girl because they never would be. Because of the stupid girl with a messed-up lip, staring back in the mirror.

Ronnie slammed the heels of her hands on either side of her reflection. She hated that face even more now. The mirror rattled on the wall. Again, Ronnie lashed out. Screaming and pounding at the peeling paint. The mirror shivered with each blow, shaking as both hands thumped around either side. Tears flowed in warm streams down her cheeks, and with one final blow, the mirror fell free from the drywall.

Ronnie watched it fall to the floor and shatter with the unmistakable shriek of broken glass. But just as it shattered, as she watched her reflection crack, she saw something else in its reflection. A figure, lying behind her, face down in the tub.

The girl... Ronnie jumped and spun around. Water fell from the showerhead in a haze of steam. Ronnie waved a hand at the blur of vapor and strained her neck over the porcelain lip of the tub.

Nothing. Only stains and a rusty faucet glared back at her.

Ronnie looked back at the broken pieces around her feet. Each jagged sliver echoed her face. She ignored them, leaving the broken pieces, too afraid to pick them up. She didn't want to see who looked back from that reflection ever again.

She untied her red shorts and reached a hand inside the pocket. The card was still there. She removed it and placed it on the counter. Red splotches soaked into the white crepe paper. Blood, she thought, and checked her hands for cuts from the broken mirror but found nothing. She ran a finger over it. Dry, faded into a familiar tint of rusted brown.

Ronnie placed a hand in her pocket again and felt something else inside. Something soft. Squishy. She pulled it out between thumb and forefinger and held it up to the light. At first glance, it looked like two short worms, dangling dead with a fresh strip of blood along their back, but the color told her otherwise.

Cherry-red.

Ronnie dropped them and reeled back in disgust.

The girl hadn't swallowed her lips. They were here—with Ronnie. In her pocket. She pressed back, staring at the red pieces and asking herself how in hell they got there?

* * *

With the sheets balled up around her in bed, Ronnie flicked the detective's card between her fingers. She stared at the name and number stamped across its surface, just below the shield and badge logo.

TERRANCE CLARKE

DETECTIVE

Ronnie picked up the phone, thumbed in the number, and hovered over the send button. She had to tell him. She had to tell someone, but who? Moreover, just what was it she was going to say? What happened in that short window of time when she nodded off?

Dental records...

The thought surged up with a fresh dose of adrenaline. She imagined herself grabbing this poor girl, biting off her lips, holding her under the water until the last shiver of movement finally ended her suffering.

She threw the phone aside and let out a scream. Its blue glow fought against the gloom of the bedroom.

She couldn't do it. This was more than just admitting that her negligence had led to someone else's death. This was murder. This was sick. She thought about the lips, still sitting in her sink. Thin strips of flesh, wilting like two sliced tomatoes.

Ronnie grabbed the phone again, wiped out the number, re-entered it, and raised a trembling finger over the round green button. She bit her own lip, letting her teeth sink in, feeling the sharp stab of pain that jolted her nervous system.

She pushed *send*.

The phone rang, stopped, and rang again. Tears clung to her eyelashes and fell in great splotches as she blinked them away.

The line clicked. Ronnie's heart skipped a beat, and she quickly pressed end to silence it. She flung the phone across the room and listened to it crack against something in the darkness.

Her body trembled with each gaping sob. She was stuck—not knowing what to do next while the guilt rose like bile in her chest. Her thin hands pulled the blankets tighter, and she collapsed into her pillows.

Each time she closed her eyes, she saw the girl. Splashing, then the feel of her cold, wet body. Smiling, then waxy and pale. Alive, then blood-soaked teeth gleaming in her torn-out face.

Just like the mirror lying in pieces on her bathroom floor, Ronnie, too, was shattered. She rolled over, trying to calm those thoughts, but instead saw a figure seated beside her bed. She wasn't alarmed, however. Somehow, Ronnie had known she was there. She had a feeling she would always be there, following her, watching from the shadows.

"I'm sorry," Ronnie said, but the figure didn't move. Even in the darkness, her teeth glittered from the dark hole of her face. "Did you hear me? I'm sorry. I didn't mean to. I didn't want this!"

The girl slumped forward. Her hair was still wet, the once chestnut brown hair now hanging like black cords around her ghostly face. "You did..." she said. The words hissed out like steam between clenched teeth. "Thish ish exactly hut you 'anted..."

Ronnie only stared. It was true. It was only a joke at first. A jealous little thought, but she thought it no less. She wanted those lips, and now she had them.

The girl leaned closer, pressing her face into Ronnie's. Her eyes rippled like two pools of moonlight, and her breath was icy cold. Ronnie shivered. Was she coming for my lips? Ronnie thought as her teeth drew near. Revenge for what I've done.

The girl opened a pale hand to reveal the lips resting in the middle of an outstretched palm.

Ronnie couldn't move. She lay frozen, trying to scream, trying to run, but her paralyzed body wouldn't let her.

Slender gray hands held a needle and thick length of thread. The girl placed a damp hand on Ronnie's head and stabbed the needle into her scarred upper lip. Ronnie could only let out a muffled yelp as the girl stitched the red strips of flesh to

Ronnie's lips. When she was done, Ronnie got exactly what she wanted, those lips, on top of her own.

*　*　*

With a wheezing gasp, Ronnie opened her eyes. Lights swirled and moved with the blaring speakers. People twisted and danced around her. Something was wrong. Ronnie got the feeling she was suddenly apart from herself.

"Are you okay?" a man asked, cupping a hand to her ear and shouting over the music. His drink balanced precariously in his hand.

Ronnie blinked at him as the club moved around her. She swallowed and tasted a chemical bitterness dripping from her nasal cavity.

"I said," he shouted again, placing a hand on the small of her back, "are you okay?"

"I'm fine," her lips said, but Ronnie wasn't the one to speak the words. Her eyes narrowed down to her lips, which moved with a life of their own. "I just need a moment," Ronnie gasped. She wasn't Ronnie then but someone else. Ronnie watched like a passenger, forced to act out inside of another's body.

She staggered out of the man's reach and into the blur of light and color. Everything swirled in her head, chemicals fogging her brain and clouding her thoughts. The how and why of her situation would have to wait.

She pushed her way through the crowd and headed towards a door in the back. The empty bathroom was as dark as the club, but the music lulled to a dull thudding of bass. She moved to the sink, turned on the faucet, and lifted cupped hands of water to her face. Each gulp held the coppery tang of blood. She looked up at the mirror and just about fell over at the sight of her reflection.

Cherry-red lips were crudely sewn on top of her own. Blood trickled from the fat holes now lined with black thread. She flexed her mouth and winced at the pain.

Music spilled in as the door slammed open, and Ronnie turned to see the man from the club barreling toward her.

"What the hell, babe?" he said. "You just goin' to leave me alone, are ya?" He grinned like a hungry wolf.

"Michael, I—" Ronnie's lips moved and spoke all by themselves.

He grabbed the small of her back and pulled her into his round belly. "Come on... Don't tell me you needed another fix. I just gave you one." He reached up and wiped away the droplet of blood clinging to her left nostril.

"It's not that. I just needed some air. That's all." Again, her lips were speaking, not her.

Then, in the mirror, Ronnie saw her there. The girl, standing in the shadows, watching with those same liquid eyes and blood-soaked teeth.

The man leaned in, and Ronnie could smell the heat of alcohol on his breath. "Remember, I give you what you want, and you give me what I want."

He leaned in to kiss her, but Ronnie turned away. Her stomach twisted as fear flared up inside her.

The man grabbed her face and twisted it toward him. "Don't tell me you've forgotten about our little arrangement?"

Ronnie stared at the girl instead of the man. This was her... Her memories, her lips—this was something she was showing Ronnie, and she knew exactly why. Because she was wrong. Her life was not perfect because of these lips, and now, Ronnie had to know just how imperfect it was.

The man pressed his face towards hers. "Damn, babe," he said, running a thumb from the tip of Ronnie's ear down to her chin. "God did something right when he gave you those lips." He reached up to touch them, and she jerked away.

The girl still watched. She drifted closer, watching as Ronnie struggled to free herself.

He gripped her tighter and moved in again to kiss her.

Ronnie tried to speak, but instead of words, her lips snarled back. They weren't hers after all. They were under another's control.

The man pressed his face toward hers.

Ronnie leaned forward, teeth itching, mouth agape, and she snapped down on his puckered lips.

He screamed, but all that escaped was a muffled grunt.

Ronnie clamped down harder, feeling him squirm like a live fish between her teeth.

He shoved at her, but with each burst of movement, each fit of panic, her teeth sank deeper into his flesh. Blood splashed onto her face, warm as sunlight, and dripped down her face and neck. Holes ripped around the pointed ridge of her teeth, tearing larger with each attempt to struggle. Ronnie craned her head back and felt the last bits of skin tear away like fat from a steak.

The man screamed through blood-soaked teeth.

Ronnie spat the chunks of flesh to the floor as the girl lurched forward. She was still wet. Her stiff hand grabbed the man and shoved him into the mirror. It cracked and spider-webbed around the blow. The girl did it again and again, slamming him into the same spot as shattered glass rained down around them.

Ronnie looked into the pieces. An image of her, wearing another's lips, reflected in a dizzying array of glass. Not her lips, no, the lips she was wearing, they pinched back in a smile. It wasn't her smile either—it was the girl's.

The room began to spin around her. Ronnie looked from the display of broken glass across the floor to the girl watching. She dropped the motionless man and moved toward Ronnie, crunching her bare feet over the jagged mirror pieces before her. Ronnie's lips still smiled as the girl reached out a cold hand and wrapped it around Ronnie's neck.

Suddenly, Ronnie's knees went weak. The lights flickered and the room spun faster. It was *her* life, and it was nothing like Ronnie imagined. The girl knew this, and was showing her, but it was too late. The two were held together then—stitched together by a thick black thread.

The dead girl traced Ronnies ear ear with a wet finger and followed her jawline to her lips. Then, she held Ronnies hand and pulled her into the darkness.

* * *

Ronnie woke in the pile of glass, clinking around her as she fumbled at her sides. She was back in her bathroom now, laying among the shattered mirror from earlier.

What happened? Ronnie thought, hoping she was dreaming.

She sat up and touched a finger to her lips. Pain jolted white-hot through her. She picked up a shattered piece of mirror from the floor and stared into her reflection.

The lips were still there. The girl's perfect lips—the ones she dreamed of having—were still sewn on top of hers. Ronnie deflated. It wasn't a dream. The visions were real—a life she initially thought was perfect yet was far from what she envisioned. She saw through this girl's eyes, smiled with her lips. Ronnie felt everything inside her: the pain this girl was living through, the horrible emotions she had shoved deep within her until it all sprung up with an unbearable pressure.

She didn't want this. She was wrong, and what she'd said, what she'd done, she wished she could take it all back. She wished she could go back to having her old surgery-scarred lips, the ones she hated. There were worse things, she realized, than being born with a cleft lip. Worse than jealousy or any self-loathing was guilt.

Ronnie looked up, and the girl hovered over her. With eyes still watery and a torn-out face, she glared at Ronnie.

"Take them back," Ronnie said, but the girl didn't flinch. She remained statue-still while Ronnie fought to keep her emotions inside. "I don't want them! Take them back!" She collapsed again, and the girl stepped forward on broken glass.

"Please..." Ronnie croaked.

The girl ran her dead fingers through Ronnie's hair. "Now you see," she hissed out her red teeth. "Now you know..."

Ronnie looked at her reflection in the surrounding pieces. How sad they all looked. How pathetic. She grabbed a long sliver, its razor edge tapering to a point, and squeezed it in her hand. "Fine," she said, holding it to the stitching on her lips. "I'll do it. I'll do it myself."

She jabbed the jagged piece inside, not into the stitches but into her own lips. The ones she was born with, the defective ones. The lips that even surgery couldn't erase. Ronnie stabbed the shard through her soft flesh and screamed in pain.

Someone knocked on the front door.

Ronnie ignored it. Crimson blood spilled around her. Slickening her hand, dripping down her chin like mercury. She could do this—cut them off and sew them on the girl's face. She screamed again, dragging the glass shard across her flesh in a quick sawing motion.

The knocks were heard once again. This time, they turned into pounding, sounding like a thump from the meaty end of a fist.

Ronnie worked faster, sawing away at flesh with quick ragged cuts as blood flooded her mouth. She circled the top lip and moved to the bottom.

The girl could only stare, but Ronnie could feel her smile.

Ronnie began to hear voices outside. Shouting, then more bangs and blows against the door.

Ronnie's lips hung in ragged strips from her face as she choked on the blood filling her mouth. She gasped and sputtered, inhaling instead the metallic liquid filling her mouth. Her lungs convulsed—she yearned for another breath, but each attempt found only more fluid instead. Soon, her chest heaved to no avail, and a kaleidoscope of colors and stars stole away her vision from the lack of oxygen.

Ronnie could no longer see, but she knew the girl was still with her, watching each tremor as she was drowning in her own blood. Drowning, just like this girl had, and now Ronnie heard her laughing through her teeth. What a fitting end for her crime, she thought. A jealous little thought at first, one she misjudged, and now, she was drowning in more than just the guilt.

She heard the door splinter. The floor vibrated under heavy footsteps.

Ronnie hoped they were too late, just like she had been for the girl. Perhaps then, she thought, she would be able to haunt them too.

***

Ronnie turned toward the footsteps marching in the direction of her stark-white hospital room. It wasn't the sound of the doctor's shoes, however, or even the nurse's for that matter. Those that always seemed to squeak on the hospital's linoleum floors as if they were designed to do so. Not like these heavy feet. Each heel strike was distinct and coming straight for her.

After a brief double knock, the door opened, and a man walked inside. It took a moment to match the face with the memory, but the card with his name stamped across the front came to mind when he gave Ronnie a wan smile.

TERRANCE CLARKE

DETECTIVE

Ronnie looked away as if she didn't notice the man.

He let out a deep sigh, pulled a chair up to the side of her gurney, and collapsed into it.

"You didn't have to come here, you know," Ronnie said, still staring at the pale blue sky beyond the window.

"Just like I didn't have to go to your apartment to check on you? Find you the way you were, and... well... you know the rest. But then again, you called me first. I heard you talking. Maybe you didn't know I could hear you, but you called, and I heard you."

Ronnie's eyes filled with tears. "So, what, you want me to say thank you, I take it? For swooping in and saving me... like I couldn't? Like I couldn't for that poor girl because I fell asleep?"

Detective Clarke leaned forward a moment and rubbed his hands together as if warming them by a fire. "Look, I know firsthand what guilt can do to someone. It will torment you. It will make you do," he paused and looked at her new surgically reattached lips, "something crazy. But you can't let those thoughts win. Your mistakes don't define you. Your scars don't define you. Mistakes happen. Freak accidents happen."

Ronnie turned toward the detective with bloodshot eyes and pierced him with a withering stare. "You know how they say you don't know someone till you walk a mile in their shoes? Or the grass isn't always greener or some shit like that? It's true, you know. I know that now! But what they don't tell you is that living with yourself afterwards is the hardest thing of all."

Detective Clarke gave her shoulder a brief squeeze, just as he had on the night it all started. "That's why I came to find you. All things heal in time, Ronnie."

Shoes squeaked through the hall outside, and soon, that shift's nurse came in with a pale-purple smile stenciled across her face.

"I better get going," he said, rising and moving toward the door. "But like I said before, we'll be in touch. I'll be back to check on you." He gave her a subtle wink before slipping out the door.

The nurse snapped on rubber gloves and dabbed a cotton swab in some pungent smelling cream. She hunched over, pressing her face close to Ronnie's while applying a liberal amount to the surgical lines surrounding her lips. "You let me know if you start feeling too much pain, honey."

Ronnie only grunted in response.

"You know," the nurse said, "that surgeon is a magician, I swear. Once this heals up, you'll never even know it happened. You might even look better than you did before all this."

"That's because they're not my lips. They put the wrong ones on."

The nurse cocked her head and smiled, still pressed close to Ronnie's face.

Ronnie liked that smile. It was far from perfect, however. Slightly lopsided and dented where her overbite pressed into her lower lip. It was colored that specific shade of mauve that

Ronnie suspected didn't exist anywhere else in nature. It was a smile you could trust—a smile of a friend.

Ronnie stared and couldn't help but wonder what it would be like to wield power like that. She wondered if sugar tasted sweeter with those lips and how they might look on her own face.

The fluorescent hospital lights flickered, and that was when the girl appeared behind her. Bloodstained teeth still gleamed through her wet cords of hair. Water puddled around her on the freshly waxed floors, and she still stared at Ronnie with those same watery eyes.

Despite the pain, a smile worked its way across Ronnie's face, and blood seeped from the wounds around it. It wasn't her smile, though. No, it was the girl's. Because they were still her lips after all.

Ronnie eased her head back and closed her eyes, just like she had before. She wasn't sure what she would find this time when she woke up. Someone screaming, a body with a torn-out face, or perhaps even a pocket full of beautifully painted mauve lips.

What she did know, however, was that the girl would be there, watching from the darkest corner of her mind, waiting to take control, and Ronnie would never let her down again.

A Life in Dust

They say your life flashes before your eyes when you die, but I know that sometimes, it gets left in the dust, too. That's what kept me at the crematorium. Not the health insurance, or the thirty-seven grand a year salary, or even the convenient two and a half mile walk to work each day.

It was the dust.

The sweet, ashy, dust.

I'm not proud to admit it, however. I know how it sounds, because normal people don't do that sort of thing. But you have to understand that it's not like I set out for it. What addict does? I discovered it by accident. A day that started like any other, I suppose.

Cleaning day, for me the new guy at the crematorium, meant I had to climb into the furnace and scrub the buildup off the walls and exhaust. Why not send the biggest guy into a confined space? My boss made sure to explain it real slow and loud; another curse of being large is that people seem to think that you're as dumb as you are tall. So anyway, there I was in the furnace, which is larger than you'd expect, but a pain in the ass no less. So I stretched across the steel tray, still warm from the self-cleaning they do beforehand, and scrubbed at a particularly stubborn clump of ash in the outlet filter.

Each breath inside the furnace was a hollow shell of the sound, but the ash itself was mesmerizing. Speckled black and gray, light as air yet stretching across every surface like a growing fungus. I traced the ashen shapes above me like puffy white clouds until I saw faces looking back at me.

It *was* a person after all—well, what was left of one after almost three hours at about two-thousand degrees anyways. So, as I waited for the faces above me to speak, I ungloved a hand and dragged my fingers across it.

The dust sloughed down into my face and eyes. I coughed, flinching away as the powder plumed around me, but with each inhale, I could feel it filling my nose and lungs.

Suddenly, everything changed.

My vision sucked in with that breath. Inhaled. Pulled in from the darkness at the edges, and my mind drifted away like a balloon.

Visions punched into me like fists. Suddenly, *I'm staring at waves lapping the shore of a lake. The man next to me smiles and comes to help my small hands on the reel. "You did it! You caught one," he says, and I smell his aftershave as he wraps his immense arms around mine.*

Darkness.

I'm riding a bike. It's cherry red with wide silver handlebars, and I feel the cool air rush past me as my tires crunch through piles of leaves. Each sound sends a jolt of excitement through my veins, and I feel free for the first time.

Darkness.

I squint into the camera flashes. I'm taller, on a stage, and I see the man smiling back at me from the front row, proud. I can still smell his aftershave.

Darkness.

Green eyes shine back at me like emeralds among white sheets. Her fingers trace my flesh.

Darkness.

She stands next to me as I look down at the headstone. She rubs my back. I only smell damp earth now.

Darkness.

Tires skid. Colors blur. Something pushes on my chest. I smell copper. It's hard to breathe. Time moves sideways. I exhale one last breath as I fade away.

Darkness.

I jerk up with a gasp and slam my head into the top of the furnace. *Reality... My life...* It all comes smashing into me like a runaway truck. The love I felt drifts away. Exhaled like that last shaking breath. And I want it back. I want more.

I stuffed clumps of the dust and ash in my pocket and climbed out. No one seemed to notice, because after all, in their eyes, I was the dumb one.

***

I craved it.

That life, that love, that last shaking breath.

Nothing seemed to work with the ashes I took home, however. I tried everything too. Eating it, smoking it, snorting it up my nose, even rubbing it in my eyes, but no visions. What I had yet to discover was that it only worked once for each person's remains.

The desire for that flush of arousal, that flash of another life, grew more inside me with each passing day. Perhaps it was because my own life felt yet-to-be lived, but either way my hands trembled at the thought of more visions. *More dust.* When I asked for training on the grinder, it made things a whole lot easier.

The grinder was used to reduce all the sizable pieces of a corpse that get left behind after the furnace. It gets thrown into the grinder and gets milled down to that fine powder everybody wants in their urn.

That sweet, ashy, dust.

It was easy to take ashes then. I didn't need much since it only worked once. I would end my shift each day, patting a pocket full of someone's loved one.

Snorting it seemed to work best, for me at least.

I like to sit in my chair, scrape the gray powder into long lines, and snort until I black out, swirling in visions of life and death. The experience was more than any chemical hallucination drug could induce. It was *inhaling* another life. It was *becoming* another person.

A person with love. A person with success. A person living until it all comes to an end in an adrenalin-filled rush.

Each time it's different.

Darkness.

My love holds my wrinkled hand as my heart slowly comes to a stop.

Darkness.

I'm spilling tears as I hold my daughter for the first time.

Darkness.

A man kisses my neck as I question my faith.

Darkness.

So many lives. So many things, marvelous things inside the souls I stuffed up my nose. Each was beautiful in its own way.

I needed more!

More dust.

I began to get greedy.

As my addiction grew, so did my boldness.

I got sloppy.

I got caught.

Getting *fired* is oddly ironic when you work at a crematorium. *We have evidence*, they said. Surveillance video. *Disturbing*, they claimed, playing the grainy black and white video of me snorting the remains of a man who liked rock-climbing, and then blacking out in the corner.

It's not like I didn't try to move on after that. I tried to kick the stuff, really, but the craving was too much to handle. I found myself watching people, wanting to see their life, wanting to see their death flash before *my* eyes. Sometimes it was a smile that sent me over the edge, and the urge to take them, burn them, and breathe in their life took over.

So that's what I did.

You have to understand, I didn't mean to do it. It just sort of happened. One minute I'm riding the bus, itching, thinking about dust, the next moment I'm carrying someone to the crematorium at night. I swear... that's *all* I remember.

The back door was easy enough to break in for a guy my size. I *do* remember *that*. And putting the body in the furnace was easy enough as well.

I couldn't wait—I was twitching with anticipation. The furnace was still hot as I climbed onto the ashes and breathed in their dust.

Darkness.

My partner tells me to be careful. Says there's weirdos out this late. I tell them not to worry.

Darkness.

A tall man with a slack face glares at me from the back of the bus. My stomach twists with unease.

Is it me?

My footsteps quicken as he follows me off the bus. His long stride catches up to me. I'm running now.

It is me.

I try to fight him. My hands flail around me.

Did they hit the switch, or me?

His hands are too large. I can't breathe. His eyes are cold as marble.

My eyes.

It's getting hot. I smell hair and sulfur.

I smell it too.

I'm burning.

I'm burning.

I jerk my head up and slam it into the top of the furnace. The contact sears my skin against the hot surface. Heat licks up around me, and I look down at the furnace door to see it's closed. I'm trapped. Trapped like the helpless person held by a man with cold, lifeless eyes.

I kick at the door, but it doesn't budge. *Who closed it?* It's impossible to tell now. Them... me... the lines between their life and mine are blurred. They are inside me though—I can feel them still—pulling my strings like I'm a marionette. This *is* what I wanted after all.

The heat intensifies, stealing my breath with its fumes.

Then it hits me.

I lay back and smile, realizing *this* is what you see in *my* dust. Not just my life passing before your eyes, but the others I've seen as well. This is my story, and only now do I see the love and wonder inside it, even if it belonged to someone else.

I let out my last breath, just like the many I had let out in visions before. It's always a relief to let go in the end. And I would know, more than anyone, that it truly is a pleasure to burn.

Tooth and Nail

J ocelyn sat on her skateboard behind the taco shop, feeling the weight of the pill in her hand. "Are you sure about this?"

Sparrow nodded. "If I can do it, you can do it too. Right?"

Jocelyn swallowed hard, glancing at the silver pliers gleaming between them.

"Trust me." Sparrow held up a middle finger to reveal the chewing gum like pink and white scar tissue where her nail used to be. "It hurts like a bitch. You're going to want something to ease the pain."

Jocelyn traced the curve of Sparrow's lips with her eyes and tossed the pill into her mouth. It was bitter, sticking to her tongue until she gathered enough spit to swallow it with considerable effort.

"Good. Now we can start." Sparrow stamped out her cigarette and licked the tip of her finger. She dipped it in the ash and traced shapes on the concrete. One with three lines and an arc between them, another as a triangle with a circle around it, and last was an X with bars on the end.

"All that's left now..." Sparrow smiled, her dark eyes glittering like wet asphalt, "is a tooth... and a nail."

Jocelyn picked up the pliers, feeling sluggish already. Was it the pill she just swallowed, or was it just nerves? Had to be nerves because pills don't work that fast... right?

"This is gonna be rad," Sparrow said.

The pliers felt clunky and awkward in Jocelyn's hand. She fumbled with them for a moment before placing the grooved teeth under the white tip of her nail on the left middle finger. Her hands trembled. Could she actually go through with something this fucked up? Sparrow *did* save her after all. A night she would try to forget. When that asshole jock wouldn't accept no for an answer and one-too-many drinks sloshed inside her. Sparrow came. She appeared from the shadows then, slashing at the prick's face, bursting blood vessels in his eye, turning it a deep shade of crimson. Sparrow was so strong then—so fierce—not like Jocelyn. But Jocelyn pressed to her side and followed her out. She would follow Sparrow anywhere after that, hoping that just a little bit of the strength might rub off on her.

And now was her chance.

But Sparrow's eyes are too alien now; her sneer too hungry for blood.

"I..." Jocelyn stuttered and dropped the pliers. "I can't."

Sparrow placed a warm hand on her shoulder. "You can't?"

Jocelyn cringed away.

"All your life you've been told what you can't do. You can't be a skater because you're a girl. Can't like girls or they'll call you a dyke. Can't hang with Sparrow and the other burnouts because all they do is smoke pot and sooner or later the whole lot of them will get locked up or buried ten-feet-deep."

Jocelyn looked up at Sparrow's angular face.

"Don't prove them right. Fuck all the parents, the teachers, the jocks, and every other asshole who ever doubted you. This is a chance to change. To become a part of something bigger. And with me on your side, we'll give the world what is has coming to it. We are the generation of change. We are the future."

Jocelyn chewed her lower lip. "Is it worth it?"

Sparrow flashed a fang and ran her tongue across it. "Totally," she said, lifting her finely sculpted brows—eyes still sparkling black beneath them.

Jocelyn picked up the pliers again and clamped them on her nail. She *could* do this. She could do anything she wanted to, and the assholes who told her otherwise would have another thing coming now. She would skate, kiss girls, and sharpen every fang in her mouth to bite the next motherfucker who wouldn't listen.

With a savage grunt, Jocelyn squeezed and twisted the pliers until the hot poker of pain seared into her finger. Still, the nail didn't budge. So she screamed, and huffed, and twisted harder until scarlet spilled from its base, and the little translucent piece popped free.

She dropped the metal tool, grinning wide as it clattered against the concrete in a warm spatter of blood.

Sparrow held her and gently lifted the wounded finger to her lips. She placed it on her tongue and closed her lips around it, sucking the tip.

The feeling—both pain and delight melding into one dizzying high—it simultaneously stole her breath and filled her veins with ice.

Suddenly, an engine roared, tires screeched, and Mike fucking Duvall stopped his jet-black pickup in front of them. "Hey!" the jock shouted as he lumbered out of the driver's side door. His eye was still glaring red beneath the brim of his hat. "You fuckin' freak! You're going to pay for what you did."

The girls jumped up. "Come on," Sparrow said, grinning from bloodstained lips and pulling at Jocelyn's hand to follow.

Their skateboards clacked to the ground and roared with the sound of cracked cement. "Over here," Sparrow pointed toward a graffiti riddled drainage tunnel behind the strip mall.

Jocelyn felt too light. The world moved and slowed with the beat of her pulse. *The pill*, she thought, pressing out her arms, trying to steady herself on her board.

Sparrow slipped into the inky darkness of the tunnel and waved an arm for Jocelyn to follow, but hopping off her board was like swimming in jelly. Every move sluggish and slowed while Sparrow moved with lightning speed. The pill coursed through her and rushed to her head on a fresh wave of adrenalin.

Mike was only two steps behind her. She could feel him there, breathing at her neck like he had that one horrible evening. Reaching for the back of her jeans or a loose strand of hair, just like before. And, just like before, Sparrow snatched Jocelyn's hand and pulled her to her side.

"Stay back," she said, nudging Jocelyn further into the darkened tunnel behind her. "Stay quiet."

Jocelyn slumped to the floor, smelling the stale heat around her and *begging* her head to stop spinning. Something moved in the surrounding darkness and Jocelyn heard a stifled giggle followed by the machine-gun pops of cracked knuckles. *It's just the drugs*, she thought, because when Sparrow's silhouette eclipsed the tunnel opening, Jocelyn swore her jaw opened too far, Sparrow's back arched too high, and her breath was too deep.

Giggles became grunts and snuffles. All at once, the darkness moved with life.

Mike's broad shoulders filled the tunnel opening. He squinted into the darkness, one red eye, one blue, flexing his hands before him. "You can't hide from me." His voice echoed. "You'll pay for what you did."

As he stepped into the darkness, Sparrow lurched forward. There was a meaty thud, and screams rushed through the tunnel like a flash flood. Then came the zippery sound of shredded clothes and the splattery drip of spilled liquid.

Sparrow peddled back, telling herself to get a grip. To ride out this bad trip because that's all this was, after all. Nothing but a bad trip like she was warned about. It had to be.

A shape formed from the darkness and wrapped a warm arm around Jocelyn. It was Sparrow, only... different. She guided Jocelyn toward the crumpled heap that used to be Mike on the tunnel floor. "Now's your chance," she said, moving the now red pliers toward Jocelyn. "We only need one more thing to finish it. To make it complete. And you already gave up a nail..."

Terror flooded Mike's eyes, but in herself, Jocelyn felt a strength she never knew before. She *could* do this. She could do whatever she fuckin' wanted to. All she needed was this one *little* thing.

A smile crept over Jocelyn's lips as she placed the metal tool in his mouth. "Just... one... tooth."

Stingers and Scratches

I was ten years old when I first heard the soft skittering of legs on the drywall. Tiny scratches that you could only hear when you held your breath. I'd lay completely still, watching my heartbeat through the gray quilted blanket while trying to pinpoint the sound. It seemed to live between the small spaces of sounds. Between the muffled voice of moving fabric or the faint whistle from my left nostril. *Surely new houses made these noises*, I reassured myself.

It *was* a new house after all. But the two-story cookie-cutter might as well have been an alien planet compared to our old home. The desert was unlike anything I'd ever seen before. Dad took away my pine and oak playground and replaced it with cactus and tumbleweed. I've heard people say they love the desert landscape, but I will never understand it. How can you find beauty in something that's only one color? *Tan.* It was too hot, too dry, and too... *new.* So, when I lay in my *new* bed, in my *new* room, all I could focus on were the *new noises.*

I tried to ignore it at first. Apart from everything, I was ten; far too old to be running to Mom and Dad, scared of the dark on our first night in our *alien* house—but the *skittering* was definitely there. It was too light to cause alarm and just as well could have been coming from the air conditioner or any one of our new appliances. Only, I knew that it wasn't.

I rolled to my back and stared up at the dark recessed light in the ceiling above while listening for the slight rattling between each breath. The rational part of my brain told me it was just an annoying thing keeping me awake, but the kid inside told me about the *monster in the wall*—taunting me with its long yellowed fingernails. I let out a deep breath and strained my ears. The noise changed. It turned from the dull rasp of drywall to the tinkering on glass. As if someone was drumming all four fingernails on a wine glass. Only whoever it was had *really, really* small fingers.

My ears focused but my eyes caught it first. The dark bulb in the ceiling above me—something was moving around it. At first, it looked like a long pointed finger, wiggling from behind the bulb. My eyes widened, watching it wiggle from the darkness above me while my body lay frozen in fear.

The small shape moved across the glass bulb until I could make out its shape. I pulled the covers up to my neck, staring at its numerous tiny legs squirming above. Its two hulking claws held out in front of it as it flexed its pointed tail.

My body trembled. It was right above me and despite my brain telling my legs what to do, they were too frightened to move. Just when I couldn't take any more, the thing fell. It flew straight at me, as if it meant to attack me in a harrowing dive maneuver. Its tan form grew larger as it fell toward me, and although it does not seem possible, I *swear* I heard it laugh.

I flinched as it landed on the side of my face. My body danced as if on fire, jumping up, smacking it off, and clawing at my face. The armored bug landed on my bedsheet and crawled across slowly with a threatening stinger poised above. I remember thinking that the scream I heard *could not* have been mine. It was far too high and shrill to have come from me.

Still, that's where Mom and Dad found me when they snapped on the light. Standing beside my bed, screaming, and watching a scorpion the size of a deck of cards crawl across my bed.

Mom wrapped an arm around me and pulled me close to her while Dad took up a broom from the hall and smashed the rounded end into its center. Its hard shell crackled as Dad pressed down atop my bed. The two front claws snapped wildly in the air as its syringe-like tail stabbed into the wooden handle again and again.

Dad let up on the handle, and we watched in horror as its front half crawled away, leaving its broken half behind. Dad jabbed it once more with a cringeworthy crunch and held it there until its many legs finally stopped twitching. My face stung from clawing at my skin, and my right ear throbbed with burning fire. I moved my hand up to touch it. It was warm, painful, and with a small pinprick where an earring would be.

What was happening? What if there are more of those... things living inside my new house? Waiting to get me.

The thought gave me the chills.

***

When the bug guy arrived the next day, I followed him from room to room watching everything he did. I wanted, no... needed, to know if he found any more of those things inside the house. I had to know what he was going to do to kill them. From our experience the night before, they seemed almost indestructible. Dad actually chopped it in half and the front half walked away.

How do you kill a bug like that? I wondered.

The bug guy bent over and traced the baseboards with his purple light. "Yeah," he said, "they can squeeze their bodies through just about any crack you can fit a credit card in." He tucked a blond hair spilling from under his baseball cap behind his ear and followed the light into the bathroom.

"So, what, you just spray 'em with that stuff and they die?" I asked, gesturing to the tube strapped to his back with a skull and crossbones on it.

"So, like, here's the thing, little man." He ran the light in and out of the cabinets. "These aren't *normal* bugs. They're tough. Tougher than a cheap steak. You can spray 'em, but it won't do anything because their exoskeletons are like, way too thick. The best way is to find 'em, and crush their abdomen. Kill 'em one by one."

The thought sent a warmth rushing to my head.

"That... and kill all the other bugs around so they move out to look for food somewhere else."

"Food? They eat other bugs?"

"Oh yeah." He smiled at me. "They grab 'em up with their claws and hit 'em with the stinger, paralyzing them. Then they eat." He snapped a hand at me like a mock claw, making me jump back.

"What happens if a person gets stung? Will they die?" I reached up and touched my throbbing ear. This was what I really wanted to ask. *Will it kill me?*

"Not the ones you got here. It's kinda like a bee sting but stronger." He moved to the closet and shone the black light on a stack of cardboard boxes. "It'll hurt like crazy, but you'll live. Well, unless you're allergic."

"How do I know if I'm allergic?" I asked as a nauseous panic rose up inside me.

"Dude, I don't know. I kill bugs; I'm not a doctor or anything." He moved the light until a bright green shape lit up under the purple glow. "Oh, man! You got one here!"

The unmistakable shape of clippers and an upturned tail burned a fluorescent green. This one seemed about the same size as the one that fell on me—it was huge! My heart started to hammer out of my chest at the sight of it.

"Whoa! That's a big one!" said the bug guy as he leaned toward it. "This one's got babies too." Its back seemed to shiver and move while holding still. Crawling over it were dozens of smaller scorpions, writhing in a mass of moving parts.

I backed toward the door, my hand holding my painful ear as I tried not to scream.

The exterminator pulled out a pair of long tweezers and grabbed the squirming beast.

This was too much for me, and I no longer wanted to know about them. All I wanted was to get as far away from them as possible.

I ran outside, brushing away the imaginary tingles and itches that felt like tiny legs moving over my body. My shirt was drenched with sweat as a cold fear shot through me. Nothing was there, but I scratched my skin raw at the thought. While I waited outside for the all clear, I already knew.

My house was filled with tiny eight legged monsters.

* * *

I must have made Mom and Dad sweep my room ten times before I felt safe enough to lie in bed. They found nothing, but the memory of that thing falling on my face replayed in my head over and over again.

"Can you check one more time, Dad?" I asked after climbing under my freshly washed sheets.

"Devon," Dad said with a look of equal parts frustration and exhaustion. "I checked, and checked, and checked. There's nothing here. You're going to be safe tonight, I swear."

I sighed. "But what if one comes in while I'm asleep? Tommy told me once that people swallow spiders in their sleep. What if one of those—"

"Nothing is going to climb in your mouth when you sleep. The exterminator got rid of them all and left glue traps all over the inside and out. There is nothing, trust me."

I nodded but my eyes walked over the walls around me. My head throbbed, and my stomach felt tight.

Just nerves, I thought.

Dad placed a hand on my shoulder. "You can always sleep with me and Mom if you are scared."

"I'm not a baby anymore, Dad. I just... Last night freaked me out is all."

Dad cracked a half smile and gave me a sideways glance. "If you change your mind, I'm sure Mom could use her little cuddle buddy."

"Dad! Come on!"

"All right, all right... goodnight, big guy," Dad said with a wink before turning out the light and leaving me alone.

He knew as well as I did that I was more than freaked out, I was terrified. Who could blame me after what happened? I could feel the warmth in my ear as I screwed up my courage and pulled the covers up to my nose before closing my eyes.

You know those nights when you are trying so hard to fall asleep that you don't quite know if you're awake or not? Sort of, in between awake and asleep. Too afraid to open your eyes to find out. That's where I was then. Somewhere in between and hoping I was asleep the whole time.

Then I heard it. The skittering was back! Only this time it was not on the drywall, it was coming from the wood floors.

I opened my eyes and jolted upright. The room, my room, felt very big, very cold, and very dark at that moment. Every black corner or stacked box became another potential hiding spot for the armored bugs. I turned my ears from one side of the room to the other, searching for any sound—searching for scorpions but nothing.

I waited, holding each breath until I heard it again. Scratches like nails on wood seemed to come from the darkness. Similar to the ones I heard the previous night, but these were louder. *These were bigger.*

The sound couldn't be coming from a bug, I thought while straining my ear, *bugs aren't that big.*

It sounded like a dog, except with extra legs. Its nails tapping against the floor. But we didn't have a dog, and I was old enough to know this was not the tree scratching against the window. I had no idea what it was, but my skin crawled as I thought of more crawling creatures, moving across me on their many tan and yellow legs. *Stinging me.* I swatted and scratched at every patch of exposed skin as my mind ran wild.

I looked up at the recessed light once more. No sign of scorpions to rain down on me.

Then the scratching on the wood floors sounded closer than ever, until it changed to the subtle tapping on metal.

The bed frame!

I opened my mouth and tried to scream, but I was still holding my breath, waiting for the sound, waiting for the thing that was under my bed. Its armored body clicked against the metal frame, and I sat trapped on top.

I moved from my crouched little ball to lying on my belly and wiggled my way to the edge of the bed as slowly and carefully as I could.

I had to see it, I had to know!

My muscles ached with anticipation as I pulled at the mattress so that I was peering over to the floor.

All I saw was the wood grain below. I finally exhaled, thinking that maybe it was just my mind playing tricks on me. The fear was making me sick.

The whole bed then shook as something moved underneath it, trying to lift it up.

This wasn't in my mind, this was real—this was huge!

A pale claw reached at me from the darkness. The oversized snipper snapped at my face from the gloom. I jumped back, climbing up onto my sweat-soaked pillows. The massive armored beast climbed on top of my bed and was moving straight for me. Its tail hovered high above its body as if tasting the air. Its many hard legs clattered together like wind chimes as it moved closer—reaching with its open claws.

I pressed back, closed my eyes, and screamed while waiting to be sliced to pieces.

What grabbed me instead were the soft fleshy hands of Mom.

"Devon!" she cried while giving me a gentle shake.

When my eyes opened, they were wet with tears. It wasn't the beady eyes of a monster, but Mom's big brown eyes staring back at me amidst the blinding light.

"It's okay, baby," I heard her say. "It's just a dream. You were having a nightmare. Everything's okay, baby." I felt her push me into her chest and rub my back.

I settled into her calming arms and let her voice wash away some of the fear.

My body ached as my heart slowed down. I was safe, I could feel it, but I struggled to open my eyes. The light was too bright, and my eyelids were too heavy.

"Devon," I heard Dad's voice beside me. "You're okay. We're here for you, son. You can go back to sleep, get some rest, okay?"

His voice was soothing, chasing away any worry. *They wouldn't let anything get to me, not like before.*

I felt Mom kiss my forehead and tuck me in as sleep overtook me like the warm blanket over me. It enveloped me, numbing my body and my thoughts until I was safely carried away by swirling colors of light.

Then I heard the clicking. Something snapping like the keys of a typewriter.

I jolted upright, hoping it was a bad dream. The dark room came into view as my eyes adjusted, shaking off the sleep. I heard it again—the clicking of hardened legs. The snapping of claws, the soft patter of something moving toward me.

I curled my legs up to my chest and looked down. A flashlight sat beside me on the bed.

The black light!

Mom and Dad must have left it for me, I thought. They knew I was having bad dreams, nightmares, and gave it to me in case I woke up again. In case I heard the noises. I grabbed the black light, feeling the cool metal in my warm hand. Holding it close, I squeezed it like a weapon—ready to take aim and strike at anything that moved.

The steps sounded again, moving cautiously closer as I tried to hold as still as possible.

I will not scream, I told myself, gathering up whatever courage I had. I held my thumb on top of the soft rubber button of the light and waited.

The clicking moved across the darkness in short bursts.

The skittering was louder—it was closer.

Still, I did not push the button.

The clicking sound moved closer until I felt it tapping on the edge of my bed again.

My thumb pressed the button on the light and pointed it at the sound coming from the foot of my bed—but nothing was there. The only thing I saw was the strange violet glow of the black light.

I leaned over the side of the bed and aimed the purple light underneath. Nothing.

"Nothing there," I said aloud, thinking it was all in my head. I laid back on my pillow. Something in my head just didn't feel right, but I chalked it up to fear. The light flashed around the room as I settled myself in, and that's when I saw it. As the light moved over my blanket, it came alive in fluorescent green.

Hundreds of small scorpions covered every square inch of the blanket on top of me. All glowing green under the black light. They crawled across my covered body with claws held in front and tails held high. A venomous ocean of moving parts ready to strike its prey.

I flung the blanket off me and ran to the door, screaming while I slapped every inch of my body. I pressed my back to the door and flipped the light switch on while feeling the phantom legs still moving across me in my mind.

Nothing happened.

I tried the light switch again, snapping it on and off—but still, nothing happened. I turned in horror to see hundreds of scorpions moving across the floor. All pointed in a single direction—toward me.

My hand reached for the door handle. It was slick with sweat as I fumbled to turn it, but as with the light switch, it did not work. The handle wouldn't turn. I looked back to see the small bugs marching closer, each tiny leg clicking across the floor, echoing in my mind.

I pulled on the door and then slammed my shoulder against it. Still, it didn't budge. The scorpions were at my feet. I tried to scream but nothing came out. The bugs formed a semicircle around me as they threatened to climb upward.

I lifted my bare foot, taking aim at the closest, and brought down my heel on top of it. The bug flattened with a sickening crunch. I lifted it up, readying to smash the next but gasped at the sight of hundreds of smaller scorpions running away from the corpse.

Babies, I thought.

As I stood there petrified, one started to move up my leg. I knocked it off with a kick and sent it flying. Reactively, I started smashing more with my heel—each time crunching down and each time more smaller scorpions went scattering from the body.

I kept smashing them but more continued to come. It was as if they were drawn to me magnetically in a never-ending stream. There were too many. They crawled up my legs and arms. Scratching at my skin.

I ran across the room, stepping over them as I moved to the farthest corner. I swatted them off my skin and shook them out of my hair, trying to rid myself of the horrible things. But just as quick as I pressed my back to the wall and looked up, they were gone.

I saw nothing but darkness across the empty floor but still, I heard them. I could hear them scratching inside my head as if they were moving over my brain. Moving behind my ear.

My ear...

I reached up to feel the sore bump, but when my hand touched it, the pain was gone. The throbbing and the bump with a pinprick in it were gone. Instead, my fingers found something else.

I prodded what felt like a hard string coming out of my ear before pinching it between my thumb and forefinger. I tried to keep from trembling as I pulled on it. The world then became a rushing wave of noise and pain, all coming from my ear. The wave of static rushed louder until it ended with a *pop*, and the pain subsided.

I turned to see what I pulled from my ear, but I already knew. Squirming between my fingers' grasp was a small, tan scorpion. I gasped as I watched its eight legs twitch and its tail reach for my fingers.

I dropped it to the floor but still I heard *more*. I could close my eyes and hear them—crawling inside my head.

***

I opened my eyes to see the exterminator circling my room with his same casual grace. I tried to blink away the fog but it still lingered in my vision with the terror of what I just experienced. As I got out of bed, he looked at me and squinted, as if searching for another scorpion. I reflexively held a hand to my ear.

The bump was gone and so was the scorpion.

Once again, I watched as he sprayed, dusted, and checked the glue traps but found nothing. As he combed the room, I suddenly realized I wasn't the only one following him. Both Mom and Dad had somehow materialized beside me, watching eagerly for some answer as to what was going on. No one said a word until he paused for a moment while walking past my bed.

"Hmm..." he grunted while turning his head in thought.

"What? What is it?" Dad shouted from behind.

He didn't answer and instead squatted down near the corner of the bed.

We leered closer, struggling to see over his shoulder as he picked at a gap in the stitching of the mattress. He shoved two gloved fingers inside before tearing the opening larger.

"Whoa!" He jumped back with a look of terror in his eyes. We turned to see what he had found but nothing could have prepared us for what he'd found. Scorpions poured out from the gaping hole of the mattress—hundreds of them. All skittering in every direction. With the hole now big enough, we could see that the mattress was filled with them. It was as if the whole thing had been stuffed with scorpions.

I watched the mass of crawling yellow bodies wiggle and thrash on top of one another, and the room started to spin. The mattress deflated as more came streaming out from inside. I backed away, hearing the scratches. Hearing the skittering. All of it moving inside my head.

The darkness at the edges of my eyes began crawling over, and the room began spinning too fast. My knees buckled, and my body hit the floor.

* * *

I heard the electronic beep of the monitor before I opened my eyes. The bright lights stung and I squinted at the white room around me. It didn't take me long to find Mom's big brown eyes looking into mine.

She did not say a word as I looked around the hospital room. She only brushed back the hair from my forehead and smiled.

Dad sat beside her and jumped at seeing me awake.

"How's the fever?" he asked, placing a heavy hand on my knee.

"Fever?" I asked.

"You've been in and out of it for a while now, baby," Mom said. "Do you remember?"

I shook my head no as she continued to brush the hair away from my forehead.

"You were stung by a scorpion. On our first night in the house. Do you remember that?"

My hand reached up for my ear. The bump with the tiny hole at its center was there. It was smaller, and the pain had lessened but once again, the rubbery flesh felt like my own.

"You went a whole day with a fever. We found you in bed, thrashing around, burning up, and rushed you to the hospital," Mom said. "Did you even know you were stung?"

"I... remember the bugs, and my ear hurting but... *stung*? The *first* night?"

She nodded before Dad answered, "Turns out you're allergic. You've been in and out of a fever for a while now. Doc says we got you here just in time. If I knew... I never would have moved us to that place. I'm sorry, Dev."

I had a hard time figuring what was real and what was merely a fever-induced nightmare for a while. What *was* clear however was that I almost died, and I would probably forever be *terrified* of scorpions for the rest of my life.

I was released from the hospital shortly after the fever was gone, and it wasn't too much longer after that we moved to a new house. One that did not have scorpions living in the walls. Despite my parents' protests, I made them get me a new mattress as well. You know... just to be safe. Now, we always make sure the exterminator is paid in full, and we haven't seen another scorpion since.

To this day though, in the quiet hours of the night, sometimes I still hear them. I hear the clicking of legs, and I *feel* the scratching of claws, as if they're moving across my brain.

Mom and Dad tell me that it's all inside my head: the sound, the scratches, all of it. But I always answer and tell them.

That's exactly what I'm afraid of.

The Nights I Die

Death doesn't come like a splash of cold water, but like the cooling of hot embers. It fades, with only an occasional stray breeze trying to reignite the flame with a breath of hope, and then fails. It's there that I wait until the last bit of warmth fades from my being.

On nights when the moon reaches its fifth cycle and paints the world gray, *I die*. The full moon brings a darkness along with it, one that takes away the thoughts and feelings of a rational man, along with his pulse. Along with *my pulse*. I panic each time it comes, gasping for the breath I know I *will not* take. I watch through cold, dead eyes as my hands begin to reach, my teeth begin to itch, and my *hunger* begins to grow. Nails scratch at the wood and plaster, wishing instead for skin and flesh.

There is no stopping it. I watch as an idle passenger while the *other* takes control. The same teeth I used to smile at the grocery store clerk, soon hunger to sink into his soft flesh. I watch my corpse drag our feet across the floor and I listen to the throaty noises escaping our mouth. I am helpless to witness the atrocities committed by my lifeless body on each full moon. I fear for whoever my corpse happens to find, whoever I am forced to watch die by my own hands and teeth.

***

The following morning, I woke up to mangled hands and a mouth full of splinters. I didn't need to see the fist-sized hole in the door to tell me what happened in the night. I knew quite well that I tore free from the straps that held me. I was just thankful that I wasn't able to get through the door again. A stomach full of the door I tried to chew through was always better than the alternative.

Despite my best efforts, the smell of rotting meat always lingered for a day or two. After buttoning a blue shirt with my name embroidered above the breast pocket, I sprayed myself with cologne before heading out the door. My split fingers fumbled to lock my apartment door before I turned to walk toward the parking garage. My neighbor came walking in my direction in slow, short strides. Her emerald eyes fixed on me as our paths almost crossed. She smiled. Even as she was just going home in her scrubs, she looked *beautiful*.

I looked away and continued past. Considering my *condition*, I *always* made a conscious effort to avoid human interaction when I could. I can't afford to get close to someone only to be forced to watch in horror as my undead body tears into them. I swore I wouldn't let *that* happen again.

I pulled my hat lower to hide my face, but while walking past I heard her greet me. My heart fluttered.

***

The tool belt felt heavier than the previous day as I tugged it around my scrawny waist. It was always heavier on days after the change. After becoming undead, then un-undead, it would always take a few days to recover back to normal. I checked the address on the service call before walking up the overgrown path to the house. The small, discolored home stood out alongside the nicer, high-end ones in the area.

The door looked like it might fall off if I knocked too hard. Still, I knocked twice and waited until it creaked open.

The man on the other side stared through the two-inch gap and yelled, "What do you want?"

His accent was thick, and I couldn't quite determine its origin.

"I have a service appointment for a cable install," I said.

He eyed me up and down. "Oh...right."

He opened the door the rest of the way. A wave of pungent incense assaulted my senses as I shuffled around the small, elderly man.

"The television is over here," he said, pointing behind the hazardous stack of crates.

I moved to the wall and found the proper line before tracing it to the conjunction. The man eyed me all the while as if I was some sort of riddle. I had squeezed behind his stacked belongings to remove a faceplate when I felt his hand on the back of my arm. His grip was surprisingly strong for an old man.

I jerked my arm away, but his hand held tight. "Hey, watch it buddy!" I shouted as his free hand grabbed mine. He turned it over, eyeing it close to his face.

His wooly brows hung low over dark eyes lined with wrinkles. He pulled me close. "I see it in you, young man. I can see..." He paused. " You walk between worlds. You are neither living nor dead."

My heart froze. I was hiding my secret for so long, and the whole time no one had figured it out. Not until then—not until *him*.

He let go and looked in my eyes as if searching my very soul. "How long?" he asked.

Without thinking, I answered, "*Too long*."

"How many?"

"*Too many*," I whispered.

The answer sent sharp memories through my mind of the nights I tried to forget.

He took a step closer before closing his eyes and inhaling deeply. I stepped back, moving closer to the door.

"There is no cure," he began, "but you *can* stop it, forever, if the suffering is too much."

My hand reached for the door and I flung it open. I wanted to get out of there, *needed* to get out of there. "I... have to go!" I called out as I backed through the door. "Y-y-you should be good to go."

He watched me from the doorway and yelled, "You will come back when you need help, young man! I only ask that you come back before it's too late!"

I sped out of there like my ass was on fire, drove a block or so, and pulled over to get my head straight. *How could he tell? How did he know?* I took my time, trying to process it all before going to the next appointment. The experience rattled me, and I was already weak from the previous night. Until now, no one had guessed my secret.

He somehow knew that I was a monster.

* * *

After making it through that particularly rough day, I couldn't wait to get back to the apartment and get some much-needed sleep. I was weaker than ever and the belly full of front door wasn't doing me any favors.

When I turned the corner toward my apartment, I was surprised to see my neighbor standing in front of my door. I stopped dead in my tracks with eyes wide enough to fall out of my head. I considered turning and leaving to avoid the interaction, but she had clearly heard me approaching, because she looked straight at me with a *perfectly* practiced smile.

"Oh, sorry," she said. "I was just knocking on your door." She slid loose strands of blonde hair behind her ear.

I walked closer but kept my eyes downcast. "Oh... ah... okay. How can I help you?" The words came out more *herky-jerky* than even *I* expected.

"I'm Bethany," she said with a giddy voice, holding her hand out to mine. "I live just across the hall from you."

I hesitated a little before reaching out my hand in return. "Elijah," I finally managed to say and jerked my hand back. My skin was still a bit gray from the night before, and I worried she would notice. I glanced up at her green eyes tentatively and melted. Even in the dim light of the hall, they somehow managed to sparkle.

"I was having problems with my TV and heard that you work for the cable company. So...I was sort of hoping you might be able to help me?" She held her hands out in a pleading motion.

Say no! Don't do it! Do not get close to her! Remember the last time!

"Sure, I can do that," I replied.

I hated myself as I followed her into her apartment, but I was powerless in front of that smile.

"Sorry for the mess," she said as I stepped inside. The apartment was a mirror image of mine, except without the scratch marks in the door. And the entire space was filled with canvases and a rainbow of spilled paint splotches. Each canvas was painted in the most brilliant of colors. Each was beautiful and bright; in fact, each was perfect!

"*Whoa...*" I said aloud as I scanned the room. "Did you paint these?"

She looked away bashfully before responding, "It's a... hobby of mine, you could say. It might sound dumb but I'm around so much pain and death at the hospital that it's nice to create something uplifting and colorful."

"I know the feeling," I said. She responded only with a confused expression. "These are *wonderful!*" I turned toward her. "*You are wonderful!*" I cursed myself again as our eyes met, sparking like flint on steel.

"Thank you," she said with a coy giggle. "Do you like art?"

"I like just about anything that's bright and hopeful. I have enough darkness and death in my life as well."

What are you doing? Leave now, before it's too late! Before something happens! But I didn't listen.

Fixing her TV was the easy part. Figuring out how to stop myself from doing what I wanted to do before the *other* did something terrible... was the hard part. We made plans for coffee before I left. I hated myself for doing it, but I did it anyway.

* * *

We hit it off almost immediately. She was witty, smart, and the most beautiful person I could imagine. We talked for hours, laughing at each other's bad jokes, getting lost in each other's eyes, and making nervous conversation about the small things in life.

I hated myself at the end of it. I hated how happy I was. I hated the monster inside me. Most of all, I hated what I had to do. My conscience caught up to me and I made up a lie when she knocked on my door the next night.

"Elijah? It's Beth," she said through my newly repaired door. "Are you busy?"

I didn't look through the peephole for fear of being hypnotized by that smile again.

"Hey, Beth," I said in the best sickly voice I could manage. "Sorry, I'm not feeling well. I might have to give you a raincheck."

"Oh... well, it's okay, I'm used to sick people. Maybe I can take care of you. I *am* a nurse, you know!"

"I know, but I would hate to be the one to get you sick," I said, really stretching the limits of my acting ability.

"Trust me, I would love to see you, even if you are—"

"Look, Beth, I'm really not up to it today. I'm sorry, but I just need to lie down." It hurt to say it, and it hurt even more when I heard the dejection in her voice.

"Okay... well... let me know if I can help. Or feel free to pop over anytime. You know where to find me."

I thanked her, but I really just wanted to pound my head into the door instead. "I'll, uh... see you soon."

The rest of the month went on like this. She stopped over a few more times to see how I was feeling, and I lied each time. I even called in to work to avoid her seeing me come and go. Soon enough, a whole week went by without a visit, and I assumed she figured out I was avoiding her. She probably thought I wasn't interested.

That was only half true.

***

The full moon came back soon enough, like it always did. I went through my usual preparations of checking the restraints, door locks, and windows until I was ready for the change. *Ready to die.*

I sat in the chair bolted to the floor and tightened the leather straps around my feet. After tightening the one over my left hand, I pulled the strap around my right one with my teeth. I left the TV on at full volume to drown out the noise. My neighbors might think I'm an asshole, but at least they wouldn't find out that I'm a... Well, *you know.*

The room went dark and my heart slowed. It was something I was familiar with, but it never got easier. It hurts every time. The ragged breaths I try to take. The thoughts that slow until they stop. The world goes black and then the other takes over.

I watch in a helpless daze the changes occurring to my body. The sounds coming from my mouth are no longer mine. The leather straps groan and flex as my body jerks against them, trying to break free. My teeth snap at the air, aching for a meal made of flesh and blood. I see all of this and am terrified, hoping for the sun to rise quickly.

The knock at the door would have stopped my heart if I weren't already dead.

"Elijah? Are you home?"

It was Beth. *Dear God, why did it have to be Beth?*

The *other* looked at the door and jerked even harder at the straps. It grunted like a pig about to feed.

"I just wanted to make sure you were okay. I haven't heard from you in awhile."

The *other* squirmed and twisted, grunting even louder. Flexing even harder.

Not Beth! Why did you come here? Why now? Fuck, I knew it eventually would come to this!

My corpse, now more excited than ever, yanked on our right arm, snapping it free with a *clang* from the breaking of the buckle.

Run, Beth! Run! I tried to scream, but all I heard were the terrible grunts of excitement.

The right hand began clawing at the left strap, fingernails tearing away the flesh around it, but the wounds didn't bleed. By a stroke of dumb luck, the dead bastard managed to claw through the strap and set the left hand free. Both hands reached for the door as we rose to our feet.

He tried to step forward but fell; the leg straps were still holding us tight. We pulled and attacked the straps until the right leg was freed in a flurry of snapping bolts and flying metal. Then we pulled on the left one until something popped like a tree branch bent too far. The limp foot wiggled free from the other restraint, and he stood and dragged the mangled foot toward the door.

I tried everything I could to stop him, to take control, but it was pointless. The grim truth was that I was no more than a prisoner locked inside my own corpse. He slammed our body against the door with no luck. He repeated this again and again, until he hit the door with enough force to send it flying from its frame.

The hall was empty. Relief washed over me only a moment before my undead body turned to an opening door across the hall. *Beth's door.* The *other* lumbered toward the noise. She poked her head out and looked at me—the same emerald eyes that knocked me dead the first time I saw them. She smiled at my corpse—the same *perfect* smile that left me powerless.

"Hey there, stranger," she said as my body shuffled nearer. "I was beginning to wonder if I would ever see you..." Her eyes widened as she spotted my gray skin and dislocated limb move into the light. "Elijah? Are you okay?"

Her face contorted as my dead, outstretched hands reached for her in her doorway. She moved to take a step back,

187

but her foot was hung up on the corner of a canvas—*that fucking canvas!*—and she fell to the floor screaming.

I tried to close my eyes, tried to look away, but I couldn't. The *other* fell on top of her and grabbed at her hand, the same hand that created the *wonderful* paintings surrounding us, and took a bite.

Blood splashed onto the *bright* and *hopeful* pictures. The once beautiful paintings were now stained with her. It was *my* claws that took her life. It was *my* teeth that quieted her hand.

I was spared any further torture when the *other* left to investigate the car alarm that blared from the parking garage. I wept inwardly, for he would not weep. I screamed behind a mouth that only moaned. I could only wait for the sun to rise and the terror to end.

* * *

The old man's house looked the same when I arrived in the night—a sunburned shanty surrounded by the fresh paint of upper middle class suburbia. I was nervous walking up the overgrown steps again. The thought of the small man looking through me like a window left me feeling naked and bare. I was afraid of what he would find when he looked into me this time.

My knuckles tapped against the chipped door and the old man answered right away. Once again, he opened the door a few inches and yelled in his odd accent, "What do you want?"

I peered into the dark crack. His eyes glittered through the gloom, and I could feel them searching me.

"I knew you would come back. I could see it in you then as I see it in you now. Only *worse*. Come in, young man, come in." He opened the door and stood aside as I shuffled in without a word. I imagine I didn't look far from the way the *other* looked. I spent the last week on the streets, too afraid to go back.

The door shut before I spoke. "You said you could help me..." My voice was shaking and almost unrecognizable.

"Come... Sit." The man gestured to a round rug with a square pillow atop it on the floor. I sat without protest as he took a seat across from me.

"I can't take it anymore," I began as he placed his wrinkled hand on his knees. "I never wanted her to get hurt. I tried to stop myself... but I was too late." My eyes welled with tears, blurring the outline of the man across from me. "I couldn't stop it! The change came and she was just... there! Then I—the *other*—took over, and I watched as I bit into her. I could feel her flesh sliding down my throat. Her blood splashing on my face..." Tears were flowing freely now.

The old man didn't move or even make a noise.

"After the sun rose, I couldn't go back there. I couldn't see what I did to her, even if I had already seen it once before. I know I was the one that did it." Using my sleeve, I wiped my nose. "I left. I've been sleeping in gutters. I've been trying to disappear, but I can't. I can't die! It won't let me! I'm already dead."

The man grunted. He turned to a weathered box behind him. At first glance, it looked like a cigar box, only it wasn't.

"There is only one way I know of," he began, "but it is a choice you must make, and a strength you must possess." His knotted fingers drummed the box like a percussion instrument.

"I'll do it! This needs to end! Every time I blink, I see her eyes, her smile... I see her blood."

"Very well," he replied, and opened the box. From it, he produced a folded black cloth and unwrapped it gingerly. A silver object emerged from the cloth, and he held the tool up before him in the dull light. It was smaller than my forearm and had a leather handle. There was one silver prong in the middle and two alongside it that angled inward until meeting at its tip.

He placed it on the rug between us and grabbed another item from the box, one which resembled a dried bundle of grass. He held it to the candle nearby and it went up in a flash of flame and smoke. He held the burning bundle as the room filled with a noxious smoke. I coughed and sputtered like an old car for a moment before the smoke became familiar, and then relaxing. The room started to vibrate as if I were watching it through the blades of a spinning fan. The haze thickened and the lines blurred. The rest came to me in waves of muted colors, pulsing with intensity.

The man was now shirtless, squatting in front of me. His chanting echoed in my mind. He was holding my hand and moving his shoulders back and forth. I struggled to focus, but it was a losing battle. The man guided me as I moved through the motions. The room spun as I held the flaming bundle. He drew lines from the ash. His chest was dripping blood. The room spun faster and faster until everything went black.

My eyes opened and I gasped. Sunlight filtered through the lingering smoke of the room like golden rays from God. My head felt lighter as I surveyed the space, looking for the man. It wasn't like the feeling of dying and coming back to life, but more of a feeling of *rebirth*.

I feel alive!

The man came from the kitchen shortly after, still shirtless and covered in ash and dried blood.

"You did it?" I asked when I caught sight of him. "You… fixed me? I'm still alive, though. I thought—"

"It is far from over. I have only prepared you for passing into the underworld. The rest will be up to you." His grim expression tore the smile from my face.

"What do I have to do?"

He picked up the glimmering tool and held it before me with both hands. "This will be your undoing. The silver will do it. When the time of your changing comes, you place it here." He touched the soft part of my neck above the collarbone with a gnarled finger. "You place it here and push it *inside*."

I held my hand to my throat. Imagining myself performing this act sent a cold spike of fear through me.

"You must do so on the full moon just before the change, when you are between worlds. Too soon, and it will not work. Too late, and you will change before the deed is done. This is the only way to release the demon inside you. You will have to die one final death. It will be a death that you do not come back from."

I stared at the silver tool offered to me while trying to slow my pulse. With a shaky hand, I took it and left. I knew I held the key to my destiny as I walked away from the old man's house. All I had to do was die one last time. As long as I could convince myself to actually go through with it.

* * *

The full moon came soon enough for me. I spent the last week in a drainage tunnel near my old apartment. A number of addicts lived in the network of tunnels underneath the city, and I felt more at home with them than anywhere else. They left me alone in my spiral of destruction, and I left them to theirs.

But the thought of *truly* dying in a drainage tunnel didn't feel right.

When the time came, I decided to go home.

Seeing the hallway brought back the rotten memory of that night as well as the pleasant ones from before. It was as if I could see Beth's perfect smile in one eye and her bloody corpse in the other. Yellow caution tape blocked the doorframe and the door behind it was propped up and screwed back onto its hinges.

It creaked open with the lightest touch. Most of my belongings were missing or had been strewn across the place. I looked to where my chair used to be and saw only four bolts sticking out from the floor to threaten the foot of any unfocused passerby. I picked up one of the overturned chairs from the kitchen and placed it over the bolts. It wasn't the same chair, but it would do. There was no need for locks and straps this time. I sat in it, facing the door, just as I did during the last full moon. My heart beat fast and loud, as if it knew it would soon stop. My hands shook as I placed the strange instrument on my lap.

The silver would do it.

I thought of only one thing while I waited for the perfect time: Bethany. If life were as it was in the movies, last month we would have eaten take-out and watched bad TV until temptation overtook us. We would have made passionate love and let the cool breeze from the window tingle our naked bodies as we held one another.

But life does not follow the fiction we create, and neither does death.

Waiting for that perfect moment between life and death is much like finding the exact point you fall asleep. You know it's coming but cannot figure out if you're already there. I pressed the silver tip of the instrument to my neck like the old man instructed. The pressure made it hard to breathe and I felt closer than ever to the change. I pushed harder on the hilt, feeling my heart slow and breathing lessen.

This is it!

I moved to flex my arms and drive the silver blade home, only my arms would not budge. Again, I moved to complete the task. I was ready and wanted to make sure that the only person who would lose their life at my hands would be me. Once again, I tried to push it in and once again, my arms would not move.

I was no longer in control. The *other* was now driving and I was trapped inside.

I waited too long! I couldn't feel it!

Whatever ritual the old man performed on me had somehow *eased* my passing, and now the monster inside was let loose with the only thing available to stop him being a poorly repaired door.

I watched my hands drop the silver instrument.

I felt my body stand.

I heard the soft knock on the door.

And, as if God had a sick sense of humor, once again someone had come to the door at the worst possible moment. I was trapped inside to bear witness. The door eased open with a groan. I could see the silhouetted figure in the doorway as it moved closer. The undead me dragged our feet forward and let out a dry moan.

The figure moved closer. I knew I could not stop what was happening, but I tried. My pale gray hands reached toward the figure as it stood only paces away. The figure moved into the beam of moonlight spilling in from the cracked window behind me. Beth's face was ashen and dull. Her skin was gray and waxy, but somehow, she still looked as *beautiful* as I remembered. Her hands stretched toward me as my own undead hands did the same for her. For once, it felt as if I was in control of my lifeless body as both our wants had lined up in perfect synchronization.

Our lifeless arms intertwined around each other, pulling our bodies together. Even in death, Beth still wore her perfectly practiced smile. Our dry lips met in the cold light of the full moon, and despite being dead, I think both our hearts began to flutter again.

* * *

In the end, I think the old man knew what he was doing. I like to think this was all some orchestrated plan on his part, but I never went back to ask. Beth moved into my apartment shortly after we finally fixed the door. It's a surreal experience, being surrounded by the bright and happy paintings after spending so much time in despair. Even more so being surrounded by the love and happiness I avoided my whole life.

She holds me in the same spot that the chair once held me and kisses my cheek. The chair, the locks, the darkness, are all long gone now. Instead, when the full moon comes, bringing our deaths along with it, our hearts beat no more, and we have each other to *devour* in the darkness.

Grandpa's Magic Wishing Box

I t wasn't the house that scared Samson, it was Grandpa. Although, the house *was* pretty scary, too. Large, old, and as secretive as a magician's sleeve. But he couldn't tell his parents that. They wouldn't understand. This was just the way it was for Christmas. His family's own tradition.

Sam pressed his forehead to the frosted window and could feel the car rattle with each bump on the road. He let out a sigh and watched his breath cling to the cold glass.

Mom twisted a shoulder over her seat and pouted her lips. She knew what was going on, even if Sam hadn't flat out said it.

"I'm sure you'll be back to playing video games with your friends in no time," she said.

"It's not that. It's just... how come we have to go to Grandpa's *every* year? Can't we just stay home for once?"

Mom twisted her head and raised both eyebrows. "It's tradition. You know how much this means to Grandpa. If we didn't go, it would break his heart."

"If he even *has* a heart," Sam said.

"And what is that supposed to mean?"

"Well... you know. For someone who loves Christmas so much, he's just so angry all the time when I'm there. All he does is look at me in that way that makes me want to squirm. Makes me feel like I did something wrong."

Sam's dad glanced up at the mirror. "You got to understand," he flexed his hands on the steering wheel, "Grandpa's been through a lot. All that time overseas, it sort of changed him. And when your grandma passed... Well, it's just too much for him to be in that big ol' house alone for the holidays. He does a lot just to have us there, and Christmas means the world to him. He cares about you more than you know, even if he's not good at showing it."

Sam sat upright but continued staring out the window.

"Aren't you at least excited to see what Santa brings for you?" Mom asked, clearly trying to change the subject.

Sam huffed out his nose. "Right... Santa."

"So now that you're nine, you're too good for all those gifts?"

"It just doesn't make sense. One guy can deliver gifts to everyone? In one night? Not to mention the whole flying reindeer thing."

Sam's mom gave another sideways glance. "You better be careful, or Santa won't bring you a thing."

"And don't let your grandfather hear that either," Sam's dad added. "He loves Christmas. And I happen to know that he's in tight with the big guy. That's why you get so loaded up every year."

This somehow sealed it for Samson. There was *no way* that if Santa were real, he would ever be friends with a grump like Grandpa. He decided right there that his parents were lying and had been for a very long time.

The car turned off the highway through a gap in the trees and Grandpa's house rose from nowhere like a pop-up in a book. Thousands of little blinking lights dotted the old house. Garlands and red bows draped between the spindly lattice of the deck. Even a snowman stood guard out front with a top hat and broom. The scene looked magical, something out of a Christmas card, except for one thing: Grandpa—standing on the porch with arms folded over his chest and a sour look on his face.

***

Even with a roaring fire, the house always seemed frigid and cavernous. Samson followed white puffs of breath to the upstairs bedrooms and claimed one as his own. Grandpa didn't say a word as he passed.

"Sam," his dad said with that 'you're going to be in trouble' tone. "Aren't you going to say hello to your grandfather?"

Sam turned and said hi to the back of his fresh buzz cut, but he didn't turn to face Sam. He seemed to only clenched his jaw at the word.

Sam shut the bedroom door and fell into the bed. The blankets, folded with military precision, smelled faintly like iodine. He lay there, wishing he were somewhere else. Even school sounded better than a frigid old house and pretending he still believed in Santa.

The floors groaned as someone headed up the stairs. Squeaking with each footfall as his parents passed to their room. He turned his head and listened to their hushed argument. He wondered if they hated it here too. They had to, he assumed, because all they did was bicker behind closed doors.

The boards squealed again. This time, it was Grandpa's feet plodding up the stairs into the hall. Sam could tell it was him on account of the firm heel strike. As if trying to squash a bug with each purposeful step. Sam froze and listened as they clopped through the hall.

Left—right—heel—toe.

The sound stopped at the door. *Sam's* door. He rolled over to stare at the dull brass handle. It didn't move. Sam watched the crack at the base of the door. Two darkened blocks of shadow sat right where feet should be. Sam swallowed hard and waited. One excruciating minute turned into two, then the shadows finally moved. Sam listened as Grandpa turned and continued down the hall.

"I hate this place," Sam said, burying his head in the pungent scent of the pillow.

***

The usual pre-Christmas family activities followed dinner, same as every year. Hot cocoa, hanging stockings, and finally, writing a letter to Santa.

"Do I really have to?" Sam asked. "Don't you think I'm a little old now?"

Mom looked at Grandpa before speaking. "It's tradition. We do this every year."

Sam groaned and pushed the paper away.

Grandpa leaned forward in his overstuffed chair and uncrossed his legs. Thick brows shaded his eyes to the point that Samson thought they weren't even there. The lines in his face seemed impossibly deeper, and when he spoke, his lips somehow refused to move. "Why don't you want to write a letter to Santa, Sam? Do you have a problem with it?" Grandpa's voice was far too calm for Sam's liking.

"Well," Sam paused to swallow. "I'm nine now and—"

"Hasn't Santa brought you *everything* you've asked for in those letters?" He leaned closer.

"Yeah... but—"

"And you've asked for quite a lot over the years, haven't you? Toys. Games. Computers..."

Sam nodded, keeping his eyes on those darkened holes where eyes should be.

"And you got *all* of those wonderful things... because you've been good. Right?" Grandpa was close enough that Sam could smell black licorice on his breath.

Again, Sam nodded, too frightened for words.

"Then... why... this year... do you *not* want to write your letter to Santa?"

Sam blinked at him. Searching for an excuse, anything that could get him out of this.

"Sam's having a hard time believing this year, Dad." Sam's father put a heavy hand on his shoulder. "I think I was that age too when I first had my doubts. One guy, delivering presents to the entire world—seems impossible, right, Sam?"

"Right," Sam said with too much breath. He let out an awkward laugh. "And the flying reindeer too."

Grandpa interlaced his fingers. "Is that so?"

Dad took the paper from Sam and gave his shoulder another squeeze. "It's okay, kiddo. If you change your mind later, let me know."

Grandpa eased back in his chair, keeping his fingers crossed in front of him. He sat there motionless and without a word for the rest of the night. Sam passed him on the way to bed, and stalled to watch the slight rise and fall of his chest to verify he was still breathing.

"Goodnight, Grandpa," Sam said as he started up the stairs, but the man didn't even grumble a response.

***

That night, Sam just couldn't fall asleep. Not because the bed smelled awful, although that wasn't helping, but he couldn't stop thinking about what happened. The strange rhythm of Grandpa's words. The overly tense moment about a letter to Santa. It was too weird. Too uncomfortable. Sam wished he had just written the stupid letter. He wished he asked Santa to get him as far away from this place as possible. He wished for other things, too.

The house moaned around him. Sam's dad said it was normal, old houses do that, but with each sound he heard, a small part of him worried it was Grandpa coming to get him.

Until it was.

Late into the night, Sam heard the clop of Grandpa's feet once again. The steady pattern—left to right, heel to toe—creaking up the stairs. How long had he been down there?

The boards squealed as he moved closer. Turning down the hall, moving slowly and steadily towards the door.

Don't stop, Sam thought. *Keep going. Just walk past and go straight to your room.*

But as Grandpa passed in front of the door, the dark blocks of shadow stopped underneath. *Grandpa* stopped. Sam pulled his blanket tighter and watched, waiting for him to pass and continue up the hall like he did earlier.

This time however, the door handle turned, and the hinges wailed.

Sam pressed his eyes shut and feigned being asleep. He trembled with nerves and the harder he tried to lie still, the more he seemed to shiver.

Grandpa walked towards the bed with his slow, purposeful strides. Left. Right. Heal. Toe.

Sam trembled with each hurried beat of his heart. The lump in his throat felt like coal.

Grandpa stopped at the bed and the room went silent.

Sam squeezed his eyes shut even harder. He wanted to open them—to see Grandpa and know just what he was doing—but was far too frightened to do so. Grandpa wheezed with each breath and Sam, once again, smelled black licorice on his breath.

"I know you're awake," Grandpa said in a chilling voice. "Get up and come with me."

Sam jumped at the sound. He jerked up to see the darkened figure looming over him. A thousand thoughts raced through his head, but Sam pushed them aside. He peeled back the covers and dangled his feet over the bed.

Grandpa turned back to the door and looked over his shoulder. "Are you coming?" he asked.

"What for? What's going on?"

"You'll see. Let's go." Grandpa continued down the hall.

Sam followed. The floor felt like ice under his bare feet. He wished he brought his slippers, but there was no going back now. Grandpa continued down the stairs.

The stairs were louder in the dark, and everything was bitter-cold. Grandpa didn't bother turning on lights, yet had no problem navigating the twisting staircase in the dark. He waited for Sam at the bottom.

"Where are we going?" Sam asked. He only then noticed Grandpa's thick jacket.

"You'll see," he responded and continued into the dark house.

Sam wrapped his arms around himself and wondered if he was taking him outside. He would freeze to death, he thought, already shivering inside. Maybe that was his plan. Maybe he was going to let Sam freeze to death outside.

"I have been to a lot of places, Sam," Grandpa said. He turned to the back of the house and continued forward with sharp steps. "I've looked Death in the eyes and was lucky enough to make out alive. Lucky enough to end up here, with this wonderful house, and my own wonderful family. Do you know, Sam, how I made it out of that hellhole?"

"N-n-no..."

Grandpa stopped in front of an old door with a cabinet beside it.

"I wished for it."

Sam hadn't seen this door or cabinet before. Grandpa pulled open a drawer and removed a flashlight. It was silver and somehow gleamed in the darkness. He opened the door to an even darker space and snapped on the flashlight. The beam cut through the dark toward another set of stairs leading down.

Sam had never seen the basement of that old house.

Grandpa waved for him to go down first and Sam stepped inside on shaky legs. He slid along the wall, trying not to scream, trying not to run, and Grandpa followed then shut the door behind him.

"In one of my darkest moments," Grandpa continued, "I learned the *real* value of a wish. Magic lives inside them, and someone showed this to me."

Sam reached the bottom of the stairs and froze, almost quite literally. He could feel his feet going numb on top of the cold grime of the compacted dirt floor. Glimpses in the flashlight's beam showed metal shelves along the basement walls. Each held an assortment of bins and boxes in no apparent order.

Grandpa walked past and waved the flashlight to follow. He stopped on the far shelf and pushed boxes and crates aside.

Sam tried to swallow the fear building in his gut, but he couldn't. This place didn't feel right. Even the air was sour. Why did he follow Grandpa down there? His parents were sleeping upstairs, but surely they would hear if he screamed... right?

Grandpa grunted with satisfaction, apparently finding what he was looking for. Sam shuddered at the sound. Grandpa lifted a small wooden crate and huffed at its bulk as he lowered it to the dirt. It let out a clink and rattle as the chains wrapping it settled against the floor. It wasn't large, maybe one foot by one foot, and although sturdy, it looked as old as Grandpa. He wiped a hand over the grime clinging to its surface and gave a brief tug on the padlock holding the chains.

Sam took a long step back.

"Come here, Sam. Come here," Grandpa growled. Something flashed across his face. Something Sam hadn't seen before. Although it was dim, with only the flashlight to see by, Sam swore he saw the corners of Grandpa's mouth turn up in a smile.

Sam took a careful step forward.

"What you said earlier, about not believing, do you mean it, Sam?"

"I... I guess so. I don't really know."

"You don't believe in flying reindeer? You don't believe in magic?"

Sam hesitated, not sure how to respond. He had no idea what was happening and what right choice of words would end this madness. "I guess not," Sam finally said.

"I want to show you something. However, you must promise not to tell a single soul about this. Even your parents. Can you promise me that, Sam?"

Sam chewed his bottom lip for a moment, then nodded.

"Okay... I want you to place your hand, right here, on the box."

Sam was slow to stretch out his hand but eventually laid his fingers on top of the splintering wood—careful not to touch the chains.

Something moved inside. It jostled the box slightly.

Sam jerked his hand away and let out a small yelp.

Grandpa laughed briefly. "That's okay," he said. "It won't hurt you." He grabbed Sam's hand and placed it back on the box. Grandpa's fingers felt boney and calloused, but he didn't resist as he laid his hand on top of his.

Sam waited for the box to move again, to hear something inside, but it never came. All Sam heard was his pulse pounding like a drum in his head. "What now?" he asked.

"Now, you make a wish."

Sam breathed in short, clipped breaths. "For what?"

Grandpa laughed again—the sound somehow more horrid than the last. "You can wish for whatever you want. You said you don't believe in magic... you don't believe in flying reindeer... Why not wish for a magic flying reindeer all your own?"

Sam blew out his breath. "Do I just say it?"

Grandpa nodded.

"Okay. I wish for a tiny, magic flying reindeer."

Grandpa's normally dark eyes went wide and lit up with wonder. Sam took a step back and waited, expecting Grandpa to do something. Then suddenly, a small light burst to life over the box. It pulsed from violet to deep blue, glowing like an ember about to explode.

Sam covered his mouth and gasped.

Grandpa clapped his hands together and laughed.

The light burned brighter until shooting off several more sparks around it. They all spun around one another, dancing in streams of light and color. Soon the lights took shape, tracing lines and curves until a tiny reindeer made of twisting energy and light floated midair before them.

Sam couldn't believe his eyes. This was all but impossible. He reached out a hand to touch it, but as his finger came near, it turned and galloped in the surrounding air. Grandpa laughed again, a cackling wheeze of a sound, and the tiny reindeer ran and jumped and soared through the air. It climbed over Sam's shoulder and galloped a circle around his head. As it returned between them, Grandpa grabbed Sam's hand and held it flat between them. The reindeer sailed down and landed in his palm. It lowered its head and pawed at his thumb.

Sam could feel it. He could feel the magic. His hand tingled as if a thousand volts of energy coursed through him. It filled him until he almost burst, scattering himself into tiny lights as well.

The small thing raised its antlers and looked Sam in the eye. Not a moment later, it fractured back into the glowing embers and swirled in several directions. The lights fizzled out, and just like that, it vanished.

Sam screamed with joy, and Grandpa placed an arm around him. Both were beaming from the experience.

Grandpa knelt down and spoke into his ear. "Magic," he said, "is real. Wishes are real. But you must always remember, Samson, that a wish can never come true, if you don't wish it first. And magic can never be real, if you don't believe."

Sam looked across the wooden box at his grandfather, and there in the basement, they smiled. "Yes, Grandpa," he said. "I think I finally understand."

*　*　*

Sam wrote his letter to Santa the next day. Christmas Eve was a bit late for it, but Sam insisted. He wrote his wish in red ink, signed the bottom, and folded the paper to quickly stuff inside an envelope. The family went sledding outside shortly after, and Grandpa was far more jovial than Sam had ever seen him. Even *he* folded himself on the saucer sled and laughed into the wind as Sam pushed him down the slope behind the house. Mom and Dad held one another and didn't bicker or even ask about that knowing wink Grandpa gave Sam.

Sam should have been happy. After all, his sour grandfather had been replaced with one who was fun, but the events of last night still stuck in his head. Sam hadn't slept a wink. All night, he thought about that weathered box. The chains that clinked as it lowered to the ground. Yes, there was the magic, and it coursed through his veins like the rush of adrenalin, but there was something else there too. The way the box jerked when he touched it. Something was inside that box, and Sam couldn't stop asking himself what it was.

Grandpa helped heave a misshapen head on top of a snowman and asked Sam to run inside to grab a carrot and scarf. Sam wiped his feet on the porch and hurried inside.

The place was quieter than ever. Sam hurried past the curving staircase and, instead of turning right at the end of the hall, Sam turned left. The closed door to the basement with the little cabinet still next to it. Sam chewed his lip for a moment while listening to the others laugh about something outside.

If he were quick, Sam reasoned, no one would notice.

He paced to the cabinet and opened the top drawer. The flashlight still gleamed silver like he remembered. Sam picked it up and snapped the beam to life. He placed his hand on the tarnished door handle and turned his ear again to listen.

Nothing.

Sam opened the door. The light did its best to cut through the darkness below, but it seemed to resist. He swallowed his nerves and eased his toe down to the first step. It groaned under his weight, and Sam flinched at the sound. Still, he pressed further. Swooping the light around the room as he continued down to the earth floor below.

The space looked the same. Nothing he remembered out of place. Sam jogged to the back shelf as if his shadow were chasing him. He didn't have long. If Grandpa knew what he was doing down there—there was no telling what he would do. Still, Sam had to do it.

He found the shelf right away and pushed aside the miscellany of things in front. The box was right where they left it. Sam almost forgot to breathe at the mere sight of it. He held the flashlight between his shoulder and ear, then reached for the wooden box with trembling hands.

The box shuddered again as he lay his fingers on it. Sam jumped back and dropped the flashlight. He quickly picked it up and aimed at it again.

Nothing moved.

Sam looked back at the door, and no one was there. He had to hurry though. He had to finish before Grandpa came to see what was taking so long.

Sam reached again for the wooden box, and this time, grabbed the chains that wrapped it. He slid the box toward him, grunting at the weight of it. It came down with a thud as he dropped it to the dirt floor. There were no markings on any side. Only gray wood—solidly constructed. Sam spotted hinges at the top and just opposite, the lock that held the chains to a latch. He tugged on the old padlock, but it didn't budge.

Sam cursed himself for not checking the cabinet for a key. Then, the idea came to him. If this truly was a magic box, one that could give him *whatever* he wanted, he could wish for one. If it were only a trick, as he hoped it was, nothing would happen.

He placed a hand on top of the box and felt the raised grain of the wood beneath. "I wish for a key..." Sam muttered. His voice hardly a whisper.

The air shifted around him. Again, a pinprick of light formed above the box. It grew and coalesced to the unmistakable shape of a key. The object glittered and pulsed with light until Sam reached for it, and it turned gold and heavy in his hand. A key made from nothing.

Sam couldn't believe it. Grandpa wasn't performing some elaborate trick last night. It was real. He didn't really want to open the box just then, but he'd come too far to turn back now. Besides, if he didn't look now, the thought of what lie inside would nag him the rest of his life.

Sam pinched the key tight in his hand and fit it into the lock. It opened at once, without him even having to turn the key. The chains unraveled and slumped to the side. The lid clicked and lifted a quarter inch. Nothing came out. Nothing moved. Sam gave the door one last look but no one was there. He tried to listen, but only heard his pulse pounding in his ears.

He swung the lid open and leaned over to glimpse inside.

A dirty felt hat sat atop waxy flesh. The head filled the entirety of the box, veiled in a thick layer of dust and grime. The gray face looked crooked. Its long nose drooped down before hooking back and to the side between its thin slits for eyes. They crinkled at the edges, frozen in some scream of pain.

Sam covered his mouth to hold back the scream. This was not magic. This was terror. Why did Grandpa have this? Why did he touch the box and make a wish? Most importantly, what in the world was it? He looked at the sharp, twisted teeth. The jagged cuts along its neck. Not cut clean off its owner's body, but presumably sawed and hacked at.

He felt sick—reached for the lid to close it—and that's when it opened its eyes. Sam shot his hand back as it turned yellowed eyes on his and coughed to life.

"*Please*," it said in a choked breath. "*Don't put me back! Don't lock me up again! You have to help me!*" The head jerked inside the box.

Sam was speechless.

"*Let me out! Before he comes back!*"

Sam spun around to check the door and looked back at the head.

"*I know what you're thinking, but you don't know what he did. How he hurt me... put me in here like this. He's exactly what you thought he was, Sam. The way you felt about him when you got here.*"

Sam thought about what his gut told him Grandpa really was. The strange stories he told. He wondered if it was true. "How did you—"

"*Please, there's not much time. He'll be back soon!*"

"I don't know how," Sam managed to say.

"You wish for it. I'll give you anything you want, Sam. I know what you wrote in that letter, Sam. I can give you what you wished for—all you have to do is let me free."

Sam opened his mouth to speak, but someone shouted from behind. "Sam! What are you doing down here?" Grandpa came thundering down the stairs.

Sam looked back at the box as the lid snapped shut. The chains wrapped around it and the lock clinked shut on its own.

"What are you doing, Sam! What did you do?" Grandpa grabbed him by the shoulders and shook him with each word.

Sam backed out of his grasp and slammed into a shelf. Dust and objects rained down around him. "Nothing. I just wanted to see it again." Sam slipped the key in his pocket. Tears trickled down his cheeks.

Grandpa looked at the box and traced the chains with his eyes. "What did you see?" he asked.

"What is it?" Sam said, stepping closer. "Why do you have it here? What is it?"

"It lies, Sam. Don't believe what it says."

"What did you do to him, Grandpa?"

"I shouldn't have taken you here." Grandpa paced the dirt floor. "I shouldn't have shown you. You weren't ready."

Sam leaned forward and placed a hand on the box. He mumbled a word, and the chains fell free.

"No!" Grandpa yelled, but it was too late.

The lid flew open, and the head cackled with laughter. Moldy hands reached up from the box and gripped its edges. It pulled its head free and locked yellow eyes on Grandpa. The rest of its body twisted and jerked free until slithering on the floor. A cloud of dust fell from its form. Tiny bells sewn to its clothes now jingled with life.

"It's not what you think!" Grandpa said as it pressed its body to his.

Sam turned and ran. He ran up the stairs, listening to Grandpa's horrible screams, the creature's horrible laughter and the ringing of bells. He slammed the door behind him and ran into the cold, still holding the key clutched in his hand.

* * *

Mom and Dad sandwiched Sam on the couch as men silently wheeled Grandpa outside. They squeezed their arms around him, telling him it wasn't his fault. Heart attacks happen, and there was nothing he could have done to stop it.

Only Sam knew the truth.

When the people cleared out, the three sat around the tree. There were no presents underneath. The same would be said the next morning. No. Not with Grandpa gone. No wrapping paper and bows spreading into the hall. No overfilled stockings. Only the cold and silence.

Mom wiped her nose on her sleeve and grabbed Sam's hand. "We found a present for you," she said, and did her best to force a smile. "I think it's okay if you open it early this year."

Sam went rigid when he saw his dad carry in the old box with a bright red bow on top. "We found this in the basement. It has your name on it." Dad said, placing the box in front of him. "We think... that's why he was down there."

Sam looked down at the box and noticed a card with his name attached on top. He plucked it free, opened it.

Sam,

Thanks for the help. As promised, I got you exactly what you wished for.

Sam let his fingers fall on the box and he felt something move inside.

"Well," Dad said. "Aren't you going to open it?"

The thing inside jerked again as Sam undid the latch. He didn't need to open it to know what was inside. He knew it was *exactly* what he wished for. Sam opened the lid and smiled. The smell of black licorice escaped from the opening. It was just what he asked for. The thing he scrawled in red ink in his letter to Santa. A magic wishing box of his own. Only this one was different.

Grandpa's head opened its eyes and locked onto Sam. It tried to scream, but nothing came out. He didn't look all that different, Sam thought. Sallow flesh drooping from his sour face. Except, the ragged cuts at the base of his neck were new. Same could be said for the blood that pooled around it.

"What is it?" Mom asked, a look of excitement in her eyes.

Sam shut the lid and closed the latch. "Oh, nothing," he said, still wearing a smile across his face. "It's just something of Grandpa's. A little piece of him... so I'll never forget him."

We Held Magic in the Woods

Everything crumbles under the unbearable weight of time, yet somehow, I never expected the old camp to do so. The air was the same, however. Just as thick as it was twenty years earlier, but everything else had broken down and shifted as the ground did its best to swallow it. Even I broke down over the years. I wondered if Robbie did, too.

Something shifted among the collapsed cabins and buildings. The steady patter of feet crunching in dirt. "I didn't think you would come," called a voice from the darkness. Robbie's voice. He came into view as a shadow, looming over me like the silhouetted treetops of the surrounding pines. The same half-smirk on his face as when we met. The same lanky gait, walking with arms like pendulums. Some things never changed, I supposed, and Robbie happened to be one of them.

I walked to the edge of what remained of the dock and waited for him to stop next to me. "A promise is a promise," I said. This moment had happened before. Long before this moment, we both stood in that exact spot. The memory is fuzzy at the edges now—a leaf in the wind that slips away as you struggle to grab at it.

"Even an *old* promise."

We looked out over the corpse of the camp; log cabins with collapsed roofs, faded signs and weed choked paths. A pang of sadness shot through me. Even the lake had dried up, leaving nothing but an overturned boat to rot in the clay.

"It was a long time ago," Robbie said. His eyes glistened with moonlight. I could see it in there, too; the camp that was. The camp we met at twenty years earlier. The camp we both wanted to burn to the ground back then but would never wish this fate upon it now. "Do you think it's still there?" he asked. He fidgeted around in his pocket until he produced a pack of cigarettes. He tapped one loose and snapped a lighter to life.

"Only one way to find out."

Robbie coughed out a laugh. "I hope to hell it isn't. I mean... shit, I hoped you wouldn't come. I hoped I would stop that damn car on the highway and turn around. I hoped it was all a dream. Like it never really happened."

He held out the lit cigarette toward me and I hesitated before I pinched it away from him. "It wasn't," I said.

"I know."

We stood there for far too long, listening to the sounds of the night. Insects chirped from bushes and reeds. Something buzzed in the trees, and a faint croaking echoed from the far side of the clearing. It all stopped as the wind whispered through the branches. It sounded strange now. It all felt wrong. A song I thought I loved, only now someone played the tune in the wrong key.

"Come on," Robbie said, clicking on his flashlight and flicking the cigarette into the mud below us. "It's getting late. Let's go."

* * *

Robbie was the one who found it.

I was sleeping in my bunk, bottom bunk in the back left corner of cabin B, when he shook me awake.

"Manny," he whispered his hot breath in my ear, trying his best to keep from waking the others. "I need to show you something."

Robbie, it seemed, never slept. He spent most nights at camp evading the counselors and digging up trouble. Trouble that he somehow always made me a part of. I couldn't blame him though, because I went along each and every time. And each and every time, I never tried to stop him.

"What's going on?" I asked, still attempting to open my eyes. "What are you doing—"

He slapped his thin hand over my mouth and pressed his eyes as wide as the lake. "Be quiet," he whispered. He waited for me to nod before his mouth pulled back in a sneer. "Get dressed and follow me. I have something to show you."

I didn't ask questions. I was a good little accomplice and did what good little accomplices do. After sliding on my shorts as quietly as a doe, I tiptoed past the rows of bunks. Boys snored and twitched while I slid through the creaky door and into the night outside. Robbie pulled me into the darkened space between cabins and ducked his head low. Still, I didn't ask what he was up to. It didn't matter anymore. I let him pull me along, chasing shadows from one blind spot to the next until we both stood at the dock.

"Okay," he said, shoving me toward the small wooden boat. "Get in quick." His head swiveled from left to right, but eyes flicked out toward the lake.

"What is it this time?" I finally asked, feigning my irritation. Still, I could hardly hide my grin. "Where in the hell are you trying to take me?"

"You'll see. Just get in and watch out for the counselors. Palmer always comes out for a smoke around midnight, and I don't need him seeing us. Not like last time."

"Is that really what time it is?" I stepped into the boat and gripped the sides as it rocked under my weight. It was old even back then, but it held true.

"Not quite midnight, but almost. Now move over."

Robbie jumped in. His mess of brown hair hung over his face as he squatted down, grabbed an ore, and shoved us out in the water.

We paddled in the darkness together, urging the tiny boat further into the night, and away from the safety of the camp. Away from the normalcy they tried to impress upon us. Away from the people we were supposed to be. It never mattered to me where we were going. All that mattered was that we came back. Most of the time on our adventures, however, I had wished we didn't.

We passed the bend of trees, out of sight from any prying eyes still back at the camp, and Robbie carefully removed one of Palmer's stolen cigarettes from his gym shorts and sparked it to life. His face flared orange among the silver moonlight. He snuffed out the flame, and his pointed features blushed as he dragged on the cigarette. He blew out the smoke and passed it to me.

"Well?" I asked, coughing out the bitter taste and passing it back. "Are you going to tell me what the hell you're trying to show me already?"

"I don't know." Robbie swiped his hair over his head. "A path... I think. On the far side of the lake. As far as I can tell, there's no other way to it."

"You don't think—"

"This might lead to that place we heard about?" He smiled and something glinted in the whites of his eyes. "Maybe."

I eased back and stared up at the night sky. Robbie paddled us further, navigating through the thick reeds and cattails. Everything felt right then, from the soft patter of the paddle hitting the water to the sloshing ripples against the side of the boat. It was otherworldly.

Weeds quickly crowded around us and we came to a grinding stop. Robbie aimed a light at a space between the trees, and there, four bone white stones glared back at us.

"We're here."

* * *

The stones looked just as they did twenty years prior. Four twisted faces staring up from the mud. Just like before, I followed Robbie through the crowding of trees. There was no joy in the adventure this time, however. No thrill of discovery. Oh no. Only the dread of what will be at the end now. I think we both knew.

"I thought about coming here sooner," Robbie finally said. "Coming to see it for myself. To, you know, make sure." He ducked below some low branches and lifted them for me to pass underneath.

"Why didn't you?" I asked.

"I didn't want to come alone. I couldn't. Besides, a promise is a promise, like you said, right?"

I let the question hang like fog until we passed through it on the claustrophobic trail.

"You never called," I said. "All this time, and I never heard a thing from you. I heard *about* you though." Each footfall crunched into the dirt like a heartbeat.

He stuttered.

He hesitated.

"It would make it real if I did," Robbie said. "What we did..."

"It *was* real."

"I know. But sometimes you can convince yourself otherwise."

Robbie stopped in the center of the trail. Before I moved to his side, I could see it beyond him. Past his dark shape, illuminated in the beam of his flashlight, I could see the lopsided house.

***

It did exist.

Both our hearts thrummed with excitement at the sight of it. Because it meant that the story was real—the place was real. The whole of the structure leaned to the right and tilted back to the left at its top. Vines and roots wrapped around the moldy wooden logs, seemingly the only thing to hold it upright at that point.

We circled it, taking in its age, the disrepair, the isolation.

"What did they say about this place?" I asked, knowing full well what they actually said.

"They said that it holds magic. The magic of the woods... It all flows to this spot. Flows through the trees and the lake and the firefly's light. It all ends up here."

"Like the heart of the forest or something... right?"

Robbie moved closer and placed a hand on its wall. He exhaled and shuddered at the touch. I did the same. I could feel it—the magic. A place clouded by dreams and the stars in our eyes. It moved through our veins with an icy chill.

The door opened before we approached it, like it knew we were coming. The wood moaned and gasped before we were even close enough to touch it.

We looked at one another and stepped inside.

Darkness made the space feel larger than it was. It was a forgotten home, still trapped in time. Everything in the place where someone left it, as if waiting for the owners who long ago abandoned it.

Robbie picked up a cup from the table. He brushed away the cobwebs and looked at me with wonder still filling his wide eyes. So many questions raced through me.

Then we heard the noises.

Just then, we heard something move inside the house. It thumped across the floorboards, and we both felt the subtle shocks of the movements like tremors to our feet.

I turned to run, but Robbie grabbed my sweat-soaked shoulder. He once again slapped his thin hand to my mouth again and stared at with those wide eyes—just as he did when he woke me.

It moved again. Scraping over the wood, something moved inside one of the neighboring rooms.

Robbie shifted toward the sound, dragging me along with him. *Fuck, he was always dragging me along by the neck of my faded camp shirt. Why did I let him? Why didn't I turn and run right then?*

A floorboard creaked under my foot.

The movement stopped. The sound went quiet.

Everything went quiet.

Robbie reached out, and with a trembling hand, he opened the door.

***

It was still there.

After all these years, two decades, and it was still there like we left it.

It was still alive.

Robbie reached out to squeeze me, but I pushed past him.

It turned toward me, the thing, angling its leathery head toward mine, watching from the space where its eyes should be. It shivered in recognition then and scrambled back to the corner, dragging the chains and shackles that held it. Even in its hunched state, it filled the space around us.

Robbie let out a disconcerted moan. Far from the excitement—*the magic*—he felt when we were young. He was different now. He was crumbling, too.

The thing flinched at the sound of us and tried to press itself deeper in the corner.

Robbie looked sickly in the moonlight reflecting from its skin. A ghost—waxy and glistening with sweat. I watched his eyes trace the shape of it, stopping at each scar, each burn, each deformation that was caused by *his* hand so long ago. Each regret he tried to forget.

"Okay..." he said with a shudder of breath. "Just like we said. It's time to let it go." Robbie removed a set of bolt cutters from his backpack and took a long step forward.

"Wait," I said, and stepped between the two.

The creature jerked. It wrapped its skeletal arms around itself and turned its back toward us. We saw its twisted featherless wings then—now only sinew and bone. Robbie flinched away from the sight.

"What are you doing?" Robbie asked. "This is what we came here to do. This is what we promised. We have to do this."

"But..." I clenched my jaw and straightened. "I'm not ready."

Robbie pinched his brow in surprise. "What? You're kidding me, right? We did what we did to him—left him here like this for all these years—it's time to let him go now. It's done." He moved to step around me, and I again shoved myself in his path.

"Not yet." I breathed deep and looked down on Robbie's well-tanned face. "You got what you wanted from him... all that time ago... I didn't."

"Is that what you think? Is that what this is all about?"

"Look at you! Look at the success you became—the easy life you had. You found it and tortured it until you got what you wanted. You got the magic you longed for... I didn't!"

"And I have to live with that. It still haunts me, Manny. What we did—"

"What *you* did! I didn't have the stomach for it back then. I didn't understand. But I do now."

"We can make it right, Manny. We can let it go."

I shook my head. "I can do it now." I quickly opened the pocketknife in my hand and stepped toward him.

Robbie grabbed me and spun me around. "No!" he shouted.

I snatched a fistful of Robbie's shirt and threw myself against him. He jerked his head away from the blade as I held it against his neck. He breathed fast and I could smell the tobacco on his breath. Slowly, he raised his hands as I pressed him harder against the warped wall. "What are you going to do, Manny? Kill me? Torture him too?"

Robbie didn't flinch, only stared at me with the same wide eyes as when we were kids, when we were friends.

I tried to blink it away, but couldn't. Somehow, as I held him to the wall in that twisted house, I saw him as the child he once was. I could see everything as it was, past and present mingled together within these walls. It was happening then as it was now, and I refused to make the same choice twice. I refused to hold it inside.

I shivered, and my eyes welled with tears. "All I would have asked for... was a friend," I said, and then jammed the knife into his neck.

Robbie fell, holding a hand to his neck as crimson spurted between his fingers. He slumped down and garbled for breath.

I, too, slumped down with him, and cried. I cried and watched him fumble, letting the warm tears roll down my cheeks as I remembered Robbie for the boy he was—before that night—before all *this*. Just a boy who wanted more. His eyes went wide and filled with wonder, just like I remembered, and I had to turn to look away.

The creature was beside me then. It shuffled to my side and watched me intently. I stared back, unable to look the other way, unable to look at Robbie's frozen stare, and the sobs overtook my body. Everything... everything I held for twenty years came out of me then, and I shook with pain on the rotted wooden floor. The creature twisted its head. It lifted the chains and bindings, shifting close enough to feel his breath on my cheek. It raised its bony fingers from shackled wrists and wiped the tears from my eyes. My face tingled with the touch, and I no sooner fell into its disfigured arms.

It held me, stroking my hair, chirping a soft cooing in my ear—until I clamped down on the chain, and finally set him free.

***

Robbie's face was a wax mask in the early morning sun. He looked out toward the orange ripples rising over the lake as, this time, I paddled us over its glassy surface.

We hoped Palmer didn't find our bunks empty in the night, but surely he would know. He always knew, and we would spend an extra night on latrine duty for our crime.

Robbie remained silent. He only pointed his face toward the sun blazing over the water as if the fire would warm his impassive face. Something was missing from him then. Something I couldn't see.

"We should come back here when we're older," I said. "We could camp, stay the night and remember how we met. All of our time at camp together. How we became friends."

Robbie gave me a wan smile and scratched at the flea bite on his neck.

Camp was still quiet as we tied the boat back to the dock, and for a moment then, I thought we'd gotten away with it. We moved between the cabins, listening as the world woke around us to begin a new day, but when I arrived at the door of Cabin B, I felt Robbie's hand slip away. When I looked back, he was gone. I had a strange feeling then that I might never see him again. Camp was funny in that way. Sometimes, you make friends and find magic in the woods together, but before you know it, everything disappears.

ABOUT THE AUTHOR

Matt Bliss is a construction worker turned speculative fiction writer from Las Vegas, Nevada. His short fiction has appeared in over forty publications in various genres and formats. When he's not writing or drinking too much coffee, he spends his time with his family, and wandering desert trails. Ill-Gotten Things is his debut story collection.

Printed in the USA
CPSIA information can be obtained
at www.ICGtesting.com
LVHW021927041124
795683LV00011B/240

9 798989 770199